AF488238

Rafts

Utunu

Rafts

ISBN 979-8-9876189-1-2
First Edition, 2023. All rights reserved.

Cover and Illustrations by Maricela Ugarte
www.maricelaugarte.com

Mapaku Village
Pflugerville, TX
mapakuvillage.com

For all those who yearn for a simpler life, and who sometimes seek an island to escape to.

Content Warning

The following work contains scenes of explicit male/male sex and deals with topics such as injury and loss. This book is intended for adults only, and reader discretion is advised.

Table of Contents

Storm

"When the gods fight, it is the mortals who suffer."
Tumari Proverb

Û, goddess of the sea, was pleased.

The waters were calm, glittering in the sun, and my catamaran bobbed gently in the waves.

I sat astride the rough-hewn logs that served as a bridge between the two slender hulls, and peered over the edge. The water was clear and bright, and refracted caustics played across the ocean floor far below. A deep breath, then another, as I recovered from my previous dive. The water that had beaded on my bare skin quickly succumbed to the sun's gaze, and it was but moments until I was practically dry.

Out here the depth was nearing my limits, but I prided myself on my diving. I could go deep and stay there for a hundred heartbeats with little difficulty, providing me plenty of time to find and collect the oysters I sought. Gripping my small net, I calmed my heart, readied my breath, and dove in once more.

I had much to prove. The catamaran above, now just two dark lines against the bright backdrop of the sky, was small and old. Its wood, once bright and sharp-cut, was now darkened and mottled with the years, smoothed by countless excursions. I liked to think its age brought wisdom—this was a boat that had been through much and would carry me well, protecting the new generation as it had done for those before me. Its use had been entrusted to me, for which I was proud.

And that is what made it feel real. It had been several moons since I'd come of age, and there had been the rituals and traditions and celebrations that transform a boy into a man. But being out on the ocean, alone, with the responsibility of bringing a catch back to the rest of the village—that is when I truly felt like I had grown, in both my own eyes and those of my tribemates.

A clump of oysters nearby caught my eye, and I swam easily over to gather them in my net. They were plentiful out here; few in my village could dive these depths, so there was much to pick from. I might need hundreds for even the smallest pearl, but that didn't matter. Without a pearl it was still an oyster, and would be a welcome addition to any feast.

The pearls themselves, well... we traded those. There were many other human villages inland who were more than happy to trade us copper, spices, and fabrics. Fishing, as always, was our most important occupation—it kept us fed, after all—but the desire for pearls helped us obtain all the things that were rare in our lands.

It was important, and I knew it. The ocean spread out before me laden with promise, and here I was with the freedom to do what I did best.

Another outcropping provided further oysters, and I grabbed those—always leaving a few behind, so that they might multiply, and so I wouldn't anger Û. I was nearing my limit, so back up to the brightness above I swam. I broke the surface and set off towards the catamaran, pushing myself up to sit back aboard its bridge. I dumped the oysters into the large, clay bowl brought along for that purpose, resting for a moment while I recovered my breath.

It was then I noticed the smudge on the horizon.

I doubted it heralded anything good, for if Aea, god of the sky, was angry, Û would get angry too. I did not wish to endanger my newfound status by taking foolish risks, and so I brought the sail to bear and let the woven web of reeds and palm fronds catch Aea's voice, setting me on course back towards the shore and my village. I was not far—I could see it in the distance, the splash of colour setting it apart from the stretch of coastline. Yet it was worrying how quickly the grey smear in the distant sky extended and expanded, resolving into churning clouds that roiled angrily as they drew closer. The sea responded in kind, my catamaran jumping as I sped shoreward, all while the clouds stretched, dark and furious, enveloping the sky until it was thick with them. The clear blue of earlier had fled, retreating into the distance, leaving only the anger behind.

Û and Aea both were stirring, and I did not want to be in the middle of their arguments.

By the time I had reached the shore and pulled the catamaran up onto the sands, the wind and waves had doubled and doubled again. I rushed up the banks to the village proper to help the others make sure all were accounted for. I myself quickly checked my mother's hut—I saw her rarely now, having undergone the manhood ritual—and she was safe, my little brother Kana in her arms. Once we confirmed no one was missing, the elders summoned those of us who were most able-bodied to the village centre.

The wind made their words hard to hear, but their declarations came as no surprise. It was clearly a *ghaftu*, one of the rare swift storms, a vessel of Aea's rage. Unlike the normal storms which could spend days in their passage and visit destruction over a huge swath, a *ghaftu* would strike suddenly, small yet easily as furious as the typhoons that sometimes struck our shores. None knew why Aea could be this angry, but we did not know the whims of the gods.

There was no time to prepare, of course. But we did what we could; several of us set out to pull the village boats further in. During past storms the sea had overflowed its banks in anger, and sometimes the swell would feast on any boats left too close.

We paired up, for it would take the strength of more than one to pull the boats far enough. Paka joined me—he was older than me by two summers and had the strength to show—and together we dragged my catamaran well up onto the banks, tying it down. Another boat followed, and by the time it was secured, the storm was fully upon us. I dimly noticed wind tear thatch from one of the huts as I went to pull a third boat to safety—there were several still loose—but Paka gestured wildly up towards the huts.

"Kunet!" he called, but the rest of his words were snatched away and lost in the fury of the wind and rain. He started towards the village, beckoning me to follow, then turned to scramble up the nearest bluff.

Uncertain, I watched him go. Glancing back at the remaining catamarans, I could see the waters pushing at them eagerly. Like the other human tribes dotting the coast, fishing was survival, and our boats were our livelihood. I thought I could do more—I could pull up another, perhaps two—so, like a fool, I stayed.

I look back at it now, that point where I stood balanced between the village and the additional boats. A decision point. I wonder sometimes what that other path held.

It was a struggle. Even though I had come of age, unlike Paka I had not gained my full growth yet, and the turbulent sea mocked my efforts. Û had grasped the third catamaran and was unwilling to part with it. It was much heavier without another to help, and as the wind and waves increased, it became clear that it was a losing battle. I was stubborn, though. It was not until the boat was torn from my grasp that I realised the futility of it.

I hugged my abraded palms close and looked around. I was alone, and the howl of the storm and the torrential downpour isolated me. Stumbling over to the nearest bluff, I gripped the sodden seagrass and pulled myself up, battling my way over to huddle against one of the larger boulders near the beach.

I soon discovered there was no true leeward side; the rain and wind seemed to come from all directions. Cowering there, the storm whirling around me, I saw how unprepared my village truly was. Even had the elders divined its approach and we had had time to plan, it would have made no difference. Something had truly angered the gods, and the storm was powerful and unrelenting, far greater than any of the storms I remembered. Above the noise of it all, there was the occasional crack of a hut's supporting post as it gave way, accompanied by faint cries, quickly snatched away by the wind. It was as if the village itself were splintering, yet I could see nothing and so could only imagine the huts' frames being ripped away, my tribemates and family dragged and torn free. There was nothing I could do, so I gripped tight to the rock as best I could and let the storm batter me, plucking at me in its attempts to pry me loose.

My entire world had shrunk—it was only my body pressed against the stone and the wind and rain around me. There was nothing else. My muscles trembled with the strain of holding on, yet the storm went on and on until my arms ached from gripping. The torrents of rain blasted clean the smears of blood my fingers left as I held on until, inevitably, I was torn free. One moment my cheek was pressed wet against the cold rock, and the next I was in Aea's grasp, to be tossed dismissively into the sea. I hit hard—the suddenness of it was bright in my mind, and I must have lost consciousness briefly. A reflexive swallow of seawater brought me back and animal panic took over, driving me to stretch frantically for the surface. I had no idea which direction it was, the churn and chaos of the waves adding to my disorientation, so I went the wrong way at first. It was not long until black spots started to press upon my vision, but finally, choking and gasping, I reached air.

I am a strong swimmer, and that helped me for a time, but the blow when I had struck the water had left me stunned and dizzy. I tasted blood flowing down my face and had trouble moving my arms; all I could do was weakly kick to keep myself up, for the water churned too heavily for me to do much else. The storm brought a darkness with it that was like night—or perhaps it was the knock I had taken, or the blood and water in my eyes. Bits of debris swirled around as well, and something scraped by my face, a hot sharpness, and I felt new wetness there. I had no concept of direction; I was being pulled and tossed, and could do little else but desperately keep myself near the surface. Dimly I could make out something in the water nearby, something large floating atop the sea, and I struggled towards it.

It was a raft, that much I could tell, and I somehow got my arms atop it. I was exhausted, and the tossing of the water caused the raft to jump and surge beneath me, knocking my chin and scrambling my senses. Kicking feebly, I tried to push myself further atop it, but I could no longer feel my arms—it was if they belonged to someone else. They would not move, and as I watched, despairing even as I flung my thoughts at them willing them to obey, they slowly slipped, sliding uselessly off the raft as it bucked beneath me.

I had come so close, only to feel the raft gradually push me away. There was nothing else I could do.

A large swell rose beneath me, but I barely noticed until I felt weightless for an eyeblink, and then my head cracked against the wood of the raft. Immediately, all went black.

I awoke, slowly, to brightness.

With awareness came pain. My body hurt all over—my head ached abominably, and my exhausted muscles clamoured for attention. The sun was intense, painfully stabbing my eyes, and I squeezed them shut against it. I was lying on my stomach, cheek pressed against something hard, rough, and damp. With some effort, I managed to lift my hand to shade my eyes.

I was lying on rough-hewn wood, and it bobbed gently beneath me. The edge of it was just out of arm's reach, and beyond that was sea. Nothing else, just the calm blue of the water and the piercing light of the sun reflecting off it. The play and sparkle of the softly undulating waves was mesmerising, and I spent several long moments simply watching before I remembered what happened.

I was upon a raft.

I sat up quickly then, to which my head immediately protested—I felt faint, and had to close my eyes and breathe deeply until it passed. Squinting against the brightness, I winced at the sight of the bruises and lacerations that covered my body. Though any bleeding had long since stopped, the red lines of myriad scrapes glistened starkly against my dark skin. I looked around. Nothing but the sun blazing in the sky, and ocean in every direction.

And the gnoll at the far corner of the raft.

It took me a moment to process this last bit of information.

I knew what gnolls were, of course. There were one or two tribes of them near my home village; I had seen them from afar, but we stayed clear of them, and they us. All I really knew about them was that they were vicious, dangerous, and bestial.

He—I think it was male, but I didn't know enough about gnolls to be sure—was sitting on the opposite corner of the raft, facing away from me, looking out towards the ocean. His form, like all his kind, was that of a large bipedal hyena, with short tawny fur covering his body, interrupted with dark brown spots. There was a distinctive mane of longer fur that travelled from the top of his head down his spine, gradually less prominent as it approached the base of his tail. He was also bigger than I was, but didn't seem as fearsomely muscled or decorated as the gnolls I had glimpsed in the past. It made him seem younger—perhaps just reaching adulthood like myself—but I couldn't be sure. Nothing adorned him except a loincloth of hide.

I honestly didn't know what to make of the situation. The gnoll exuded a physicality that frightened me, and here I was, in the middle of nowhere with nowhere to go, and this gnoll was a stride or two away. Could I even defend myself? I was suddenly reminded, and checked my own loincloth at my hip—my waterskin was there, intact, and miraculously my bronze knife was still in the leather sheath at my belt. As I took stock of my belongings, I noticed the gnoll shift position, and his head turned my way.

His face was quintessential hyena: the strongly defined muzzle, the uniquely shaped ears, the amber eyes. I met his gaze nervously. He sat there, his arms braced behind him supporting his weight. His right leg stretched out on the deck in front of him, the other he had folded with its knee upwards. He nodded at me then, and spoke a few guttural words which I did not understand. I told him so in my own tongue, and though his ears twitched at it he shook his head, clearly unaware of what my words meant.

Taking the waterskin from my belt, I drank a little. Not much though, for I understood the danger of the situation. At my village it often rained in the afternoons, but it could not be relied upon, and I had been warned many times in my childhood of the dangers and agonising temptation of saltwater. The gnoll watched me drink, so after a moment's thought I shifted closer and held the waterskin out to him. He took it, and the brief touch brushing against my skin brought back all the stories I had heard of regarding gnolls and their violent nature; it almost made me scuttle back to my corner of the raft. Nevertheless, I still retreated out of arm's length, watching him warily.

He drank, but measuredly, and extended the waterskin back to me. When he tried to shift so that he could reach, pain crossed his features, so I leaned forward and took it from him. I eyed him curiously, and that's when I realised he was hurt. Gnoll legs are shaped differently than human ones, more like an animal's, and as I studied him I could see that his outstretched leg was damaged. There was a kink at his knee that shouldn't have been there, and once I had pinpointed it I could see how wrong it was.

I looked up at him and saw him watching me. Staring at his injury was clearly not my best idea, as his lip lifted in a warning snarl. I attempted to look non-threatening, retreating once more to my corner.

I wondered how much time had passed. Clearly the *ghaftu* was long past—the sea was bright and calm—and the sun's movement indicated morning. A day then? Perhaps longer, I had no way of knowing for certain. And all that time I had been unconscious within reach of a gnoll.

I assumed he was the owner of the raft; we did not use rafts in my village, just the catamarans, and the times I'd seen gnolls in the distance had been upon rafts near the shore. I had kept my distance, of course, so it was difficult to be sure.

The storm would have struck the nearby gnoll villages too, and based on his injury, he was likely a casualty of its fury. I glanced briefly over—not directly, so as not to anger him—but he was no longer looking my way. His head was lowered, muzzle open and panting softly, and his ears were flat. Occasionally a muted whimper would escape.

He had not tossed me from his raft, that much was clear. There could be a nefarious reason for that—was I food?—but I did appreciate still being alive, and I wanted to show that.

So I shifted closer.

His knee was dislocated, I could see that now. Much of the gnoll's lower leg was swollen, and accompanying the injury to the knee was a severe, deep gash above it, where I caught a glimpse of white bone. There was little I could do to fix any possible fractures, especially on a bobbing raft with no supplies, but I could correct his dislocated knee. If he'd let me.

He was watching me again. I had helped to set a dislocation before, so I pointed to his outstretched leg and placed my fists together as if they were striking each other, then shifted them slightly so they were offset. I then shifted them back with a quick motion, so that my arms made one long unbroken line. He seemed to understand, also pointing to his leg and making the sharp gesture of aligning it like I had, and leaned back on his elbows. His ears were flat against his head, his muzzle parted in a snarl, which did nothing for my confidence. I inched closer, and gently laid my hands on his leg, being careful not to touch the deeper wound. He let loose a low growl which he then stifled; it was clear the prospect of my help was warring with the need to set the knee properly. I watched him, trying to look more comfortable than I felt, even as I realised he could probably smell my fear.

Tentatively, I moved my hands next to the injury, and softly probed. A growl, and a hissed intake of breath, but no other movement, so I prodded as best I could to determine how it needed to be set. The massive cut in his leg oozed blood, and I tried to ignore it as I examined his knee. I placed my hands where they needed to be, braced myself, and after a final glance at him for confirmation I pushed, hard. He cried out, an agonised yelp, and he collapsed, his head thudding against the raft. A brief glance confirmed his leg seemed straight again, and I breathed a sigh of relief. I didn't want to have to try that again.

The gnoll appeared to have passed out, which was perhaps a blessing. I am ashamed to have thought of it, but at that moment I wondered if I should slay him with my knife. He was helpless, injured, and unarmed. But it was only a brief thought; he had allowed me on the raft, after all. I decided I would not attack him unless he attacked me first. I watched him for a while, curiously, for I had never seen a gnoll this close before. Even unconscious his form was fearsome—he was well-muscled, furred, and large, and his slightly parted jaws revealed a truly impressive set of teeth. I decided that distancing myself wasn't a bad idea, so I retreated back to the other side of the raft.

When I awoke, the sun was setting, painting the sky with pinks and oranges. The sea was still, as if the fight between Û and Aea had never occurred. I did not recall falling asleep—I must have been more exhausted than I realised. The gnoll was where I had left him, but awake and watching me, and the sunset reflected in his amber eyes. I nodded to him warily, but he did not move. My stomach growled, and one of the gnoll's ears flicked in response. I was famished. I removed the waterskin from my belt and set it down, as well as the knife sheath. Taking the blade, I lowered myself into the water off the side of the raft, eyeing the gnoll as I did so. He just continued to stare in my direction, which was unnerving, so I looked away and dove beneath the surface.

As I said earlier, I am a strong swimmer. And I'd fished this way, too. Granted, I would normally use a spear, but I was confident that the knife would prove sufficient. I soon determined that it wasn't that simple. It took me longer; not only were there fewer fish near the surface in the deeper ocean, but it required far more patience to come within striking distance. The sun had slipped beneath the horizon by the time I had any success, and even then it was the size of catch I'd normally return to the sea. Anything, though, would be better than going hungry. The fish was of a kind unfamiliar to me, colourfully striped, and it was still weakly thrashing on the knife by the time I returned to the edge of the raft, and I shifted hand over hand around the side until I was closer to the gnoll. I cut it in half and placed a portion within his reach, put the other half on my side of the raft, then returned beneath the waves in the hopes of finding another. It was not long before it was too dark for me to continue, and so I found myself back atop the raft, eating a few bites from my half of the fish.

I looked over at him. His fish was gone, and he watched me quietly, his eyes bright even in the darkening dusk. I thought for a moment and, deciding that a hungry Kunet was less problematic than a hungry gnoll, approached him and held out the other half. He carefully took it, stating something in his tongue. It sounded appreciative, so I smiled at him and nodded. There was little left in my waterskin, so I limited myself to a sip, nothing more. The gnoll still faced me, saying nothing. I handed it to him and was happy to see he drank no more than I had done; it was clear he understood the danger we were in.

I sat awake a while, watching as the stars dotted the sky. My companion remained quiet, unmoving in his corner of our make-shift raft, although occasionally his involuntary noises of pain, unsuccessfully stifled, broke the silence. Eventually I laid back, hands behind my head, and was lulled to sleep by the soft night breeze and the lapping of the water.

The sun was up when I awoke, and I finally felt refreshed. I still had the myriad aches and pains from being tossed about by the storm, but my cuts were healing, and at least the intense tiredness had departed. My throat was dry, but hardly any water remained. I glanced over at the gnoll, but it seemed he was asleep. A brief examination of the horizon yielded nothing but ocean in every direction, and I sighed. I considered fishing again, but knew that

I would just tire myself, which would likely make me need more water. And that was something I could ill afford. So I sat, and let my mind drift.

Guiltily, I wondered how my tribemates fared. I had given them little thought since the storm, the immediacy of survival and the presence of a gnoll having occupied my focus. Had the gods spared my village? Vividly, I recalled the brief snatches of sound during the storm, and knew that it was likely much had been lost. Kana's scared face stuck in my mind, and I wondered if any of the cries I had heard were his. Even if they had survived, they would need to rebuild. But I had no way of knowing. I had no idea where at sea we were, or which direction my village was, if anything even remained.

Hours passed, and the sun burned down on us both. There had been occasional whimpers coming from the gnoll's direction, and looking over at him it appeared he was dreaming. I didn't envy him his dreams—he sounded woefully distressed, and I stood up, purposefully making more noise than necessary as I unstoppered my waterskin. It was clear something was wrong. I walked to him and knelt down, tentatively putting a hand against his face, ready to jump away should he lash out. He was obviously feverish—the heat where I touched him was clearly not just from the sun warming his fur.

I sat there, uncertain. It might be infection, something I could do nothing about; should I waste water on him? His muzzle was parted slightly, and his soft, plaintive, delirious cries—so at odds with such a large, formidable creature—were painful to hear. I put the stopper back in the waterskin and tried to sit him up. He was unresistant but heavy, and it took some doing, but I didn't want him to choke when I tried to offer him water. His eyes remained closed and he continued to whimper, but he managed to swallow. I watched resignedly as most of it dribbled down his muzzle, but told myself it likely wouldn't matter. We would either find water or we wouldn't.

The afternoon had water find us, at least briefly. The rain didn't last as long as I would have hoped, but I did my utmost to collect as much of it as I could. I stripped off my loincloth and spread it out like a shallow bowl to try and catch more as it fell. It was made of a soft leather, so the water would not just soak through and disappear, but even with that I only managed half a waterskin's worth. I felt reinvigorated enough, however, to try my hand at fishing once again.

I did not travel very far nor very deep; I had heard tales of the various sea creatures that resided in the deeper ocean, and I had no wish to encounter any of them. My efforts resulted in, again, one single fish. Like the first, it was not large, but I split it into two when I got back to the raft.

The gnoll was quiet and seemed to be asleep. I made my way across the raft over to him, fish in hand, and reached out to prod him gently on the shoulder.

He jerked suddenly, ears back, and the crest of fur from his head down his back stood erect as he snarled and lashed out. His teeth snapped where my arm had been—panicked, I had pulled away, and felt the heat of his breath as he lunged. Next thing I knew, I was in the water. Fear had caused me to back away as quickly as I could, and I had tumbled off the edge of the raft. Spluttering, I made my way to the furthest point from the gnoll and scrambled back up onto the raft.

He was still faintly snarling, tossing his head, but his eyes were closed. Delirium, most likely. Even so, I had no wish to be defenceless should he decide to attack. I reached for my knife.

Only it wasn't there. In shock I desperately scanned the raft, but it was gone. I'd had it in hand when I cut the fish, but I did not recall sheathing it. With dawning despair, I realised I must have dropped it in the water when I panicked. Immediately, I dived to search. It was hopeless, however, for I knew the knife would have already sunk further than I could reach. I looked anyhow. After all, it was the only weapon I had.

Eventually, dejectedly, I returned to the raft. The gnoll was asleep again, whimpering quietly to himself. The half of the fish I had dropped near him was untouched, so I quietly stole over to take it for myself—after all, no point letting it go to waste. And, well, I no longer had a way of getting more. I ate it quickly, sipped conservatively from my waterskin, and curled up on my corner of the raft as the sun set. It took a long time for me to finally get to sleep.

It was strange; there was nothing to do, yet I don't remember being bored. I don't recall thinking much of anything at all during those days at sea. It may have been residual shock, or perhaps resignation, I don't know. I do know I was woefully unprepared for the situation I was in, and had little option but to ride it out and see where I ended up. I assumed the gnoll's lunge towards me was a result of delirium, not any personal aggressiveness, so I eventually steeled myself enough to approach him again. The days consisted of partitioning out the remaining water as best I could between the two of us, and it wasn't much. The gnoll remained semi-conscious and suffering, and I am not sure if he knew I was even there, but I did my best to cool him off in the heat of the day by splashing seawater over his feverish body. I don't know if it helped. I was hungry, but that remained in the back of my mind, easily overpowered by thirst. It did not rain again, and by the next day the little water we had was gone. So it was after a couple days without, bleary and occasionally hallucinating, that I spotted a smudge in the distance.

It continued to impinge upon my vision, even as I struggled to focus. Whether imaginary or not, I couldn't let a possible opportunity pass me by, so I slipped my weakened body into the sea beside the raft and began to swim, pushing the raft in front of me towards the distant blur on the horizon.

Shore

"The ocean is painted with islands, much like the sky with stars. They are countless."
Tumari Proverb

I don't even remember that swim. I was desperately thirsty and exhausted, and all I recall is starting out, making for that greenish smudge in the distance, and then my feet brushing against sand. I stood there a moment, waves bumping my thighs, staring. A beach of white sand stretched before me, bordered further in by the vibrant greens of a rainforest. I looked to my left and right; the beach travelled a ways in both directions, but was soon lost as it followed the curve of the coastline, hidden behind a variety of trees and vegetation. My legs suddenly started to cramp, and my attention was brought back to the raft and my companion. I pushed it up onto the soft sands as best I could—which wasn't far in my state—and shakily walked around to the gnoll. He still appeared to be unconscious, so I bent to lift him under his arms and staggered backwards with him in tow. I stumbled several times and kept having to rest to let the cramping pass, but eventually I got him far enough so that the water wouldn't be a danger. He whimpered during the process, and I winced as his injured leg dragged across the sand, but there was little else I could do.

The gods have always seemed aloof and impersonal. In my village we always respected them, of course, for they made the world and still guide it through its changes, but we understood that our lives and troubles are often beneath their notice. They are so far beyond us with their own trials and conflicts and priorities that I doubted they heard us much anymore. The *ghaftu* that struck our village seemed proof of that. Generally, I would leave such philosophising to our elders—they knew far more about the gods than I did. But today, once more upon solid ground, thirsty and exhausted but alive... I wondered.

Because it started to rain.

Was it a blessing from Aea? I don't know. I laughed then, taking off my loincloth and spreading it out, trying to catch as much as I possibly could. And even when the rain had passed, when I wandered a little way down the beach, I saw tiny pools of water occupying shallow depressions in rocks near the jungle. I drank as much as I could from them after filling the waterskin, then walked back to the gnoll to give him as much as I could from it. He seemed semi-conscious, perhaps due to the pain of being dragged, but it meant he could drink. He only managed to swallow a little bit, but it did not matter—there was more! I ran to refill it, slowing to a stagger as my legs started to cramp again, but that did not dampen my mood. Four separate times I did this, until I could barely move, but I hoped it would be enough. He appeared unaware of things, perhaps the fevered delirium remained, but I think his body's thirst was at least temporarily slaked.

I laid down in the soft sand and let the exhaustion take me.

The pink of dawn greeted me as I woke. I just laid there for a while, revelling in the fact I was still alive, even if I didn't know what this land might hold for me—for us, I realised, as I looked over to check on my companion. But I immediately noticed something missing as I sat up; the raft was gone. Apparently, I had not pulled it up far enough on the sand and it had floated away with the tide. I suppose I should have felt more of a sense of loss by that, but I was just glad that our days upon the ocean were over, at least for now. I didn't know what awaited me here, but I'd deal with that as it came.

The raft may have been gone, but the gnoll wasn't. In fact, he was sitting up, looking at me with that unnerving stare. Whatever delirium had ailed him seemed like it had passed, and even though I was still somewhat afraid and wary of him, I was glad to see he had survived. I couldn't help but smile at him in an acknowledgement of our shared success, then got to my feet and walked over. He watched me approach, his expression betraying little, but when I handed him the waterskin...something broke. He started to cry, tears making dark lines in his fur, and I sat there dumb and uncertain, the waterskin halfway between us both. I didn't even imagine that gnolls could react this way, and, at a loss, I set the waterskin down next to him and backed away. He didn't touch it to start with, just looked at it then back up at me, and a torrent of words spilled forth. I had absolutely no idea what he was saying; it was full of consonants and aspirants and tones and clicks and musicality and growls and I let the waves of unintelligible sounds wash over me, confused as to how to respond.

"Water?" I asked, not knowing what else to say, and gestured towards the waterskin.

He paused, ears perked forward, and picked it up.

"Water," I confirmed, and he watched me, with his tear-streaked face turned towards me while he drank.

He drank carefully, an acknowledgement of his weakened state. Eventually he drained the skin and held it out to me. "Water," he stated, with a very passable pronunciation, and I smiled as I reached out to take it.

He grasped my hand with his own. Surprised, I tugged, but he held me fast, meeting my gaze directly. The strength in his grip, the press of his hand against my own, the imprint of his claws against my skin—my breath hitched in fear, and I started to panic. With my free hand I felt around the tie of my loincloth for my belt knife, but it wasn't there, of course—I had lost it days ago in the depths of the ocean. He started to speak again in earnest, and though I understood none of it, his intensity was such that I couldn't look away. He paused after a moment, his eyes searching my face. I think he scented my fear, for he looked somewhat abashed, and his ears and muzzle lowered slightly as he released my hand. I pride myself that I didn't flee from him then and there. Instead, I looked at the now empty waterskin he had left in my hand, then nervously over at him.

"Water?" I asked. He grinned, revealing a frightening set of sharp white teeth which did nothing for my nerves, and repeated the word back to me. It had been the previous afternoon that it had rained, but I assumed that a number of the small pools still remained so I set out in search. It gave me something to do, at least; I had no idea how to respond to the gnoll otherwise, and to be honest, he frightened me. So I embraced the opportunity to be alone and explore a little more of my surroundings.

My first concern was food. Not so much whether there was food, but that I had the tools to obtain it. I had always had a talent for spearfishing, but, well, obviously I needed a spear. So, I ventured off the sands and delved into the rainforest beyond. Most of the plants—along with the various lizards and birds I spotted—were quite familiar to me as being indigenous to the areas around my village.

I made note of a few coconut trees—they weren't common, but there were one or two, and the shells would make do as water containers beyond the one waterskin between us both. Breadfruit trees also appeared to be quite frequent, and I was pleased at this; it was another source of food besides the ocean, and its wood was used by my village to make catamarans.

I also found some herbs I recognised that looked as if they'd be of use, at least for the gnoll's injuries. I felt we had come this far, and he hadn't tossed me from his raft, so I would do my best to help him heal. His open leg wound was a concern, as was the dislocated area, but I managed to find some aloe to help speed the healing, as well as some kava to calm him during the process of attending to the wound. I was surprised to also find some nightroot—a powerful sedative that is fatal in large doses, but if used carefully it is a strong painkiller. I gathered some of that too, knowing that the gnoll's injuries had to be causing him quite a bit of discomfort.

A length of sturdy wood, usable for a spear shaft, soon followed, though it took me some doing to break it off in my still weakened state. My lack of knife would make sharpening difficult, so I spent some time searching for a stone that might make do. The best I found wasn't much and would be only a fraction as effective as my knife, but it was better than nothing.

With my newfound items I made my way back over to my companion. He tilted his head curiously as I approached, and at his inquisitive expression I showed him the length of wood. "Spear!"

I stated, using the wood to make a stabbing motion, then making as if I were striking one end with the sharp edge of the rock.

"Spear!" pronounced the gnoll, grinning, and held out his hands towards me.

It took me a moment to realise he was requesting the items, but I was uncertain. I would be effectively giving him more weapons, but then again, his leg was damaged. I handed them over, still keeping a healthy distance between us both, and I guiltily hoped the pause in my decision wasn't too obvious. He had made no show of aggression towards me, after all, and I hoped that would continue when he was hale again and no longer needed my aid. With rock in hand, he immediately set to work, beginning to deftly sharpen one end of the wood. I set the herbs and roots down and made my way back into the forest.

I had found appropriate wood for a spear shaft, which meant I could also find strong enough wood for a splint. My searching didn't take me long, and soon I had a few sturdy pieces that seemed like they would do the job. I grabbed some leaves and grasses for cushioning and made my way back up the beach. He was still busy sharpening, and the smile he flashed my way made me think of him as much more like me than I had previously assumed, based on what I had been told about the gnolls that had lived nearby. I was still wary, of course, but I liked to think that maybe he wouldn't consider me prey once he had gained the upper hand—I certainly didn't want to entertain the thought. So, I took my sticks and my leaves and my grass and I went to sit near him. Not too close, though. Still out of arm's reach.

When I thought more about it, most of what I knew of gnolls was based off of a rather old singular event that occurred to one of our hunting parties. There was a run-in with a group of gnolls while game hunting, where misunderstanding and the lack of a common language resulted in our senior hunter Omo's death and severe injuries amongst the rest of the party. From what I recalled, several gnolls had been hurt too. Since then, we had made every attempt to avoid them and they us; any of the minimal trading we might have had at that point was stopped.

My silence had not gone unnoticed—the gnoll looked over at me curiously, and then: "Spear!" His excitement was infectious, and I smiled as he continued his efforts at sharpening. I crouched there with my sticks and watched him for a moment, until finally he realised that I was holding all these other items. He put the rock and rudimentary spear down, looked at me, then the sticks, and then spouted a string of unintelligible words. It sounded like a question, so I held up the sticks and then mimed placing them parallel to his leg. He seemed to understand; his ears flattened slightly, I assumed at the prospect of the associated pain, so I showed him the herbs I had found, pointing to the obvious wound in his leg. He looked puzzled at those, so I took them over to the edge of the rainforest. There was a large rock there, and I used it as a makeshift table against which I could mash the kava and nightroot into a usable paste, while the aloe I left—I would use that once the others had taken effect. The sharp tang of crushed herbs had the distinctive scents I remembered. I glanced back at the gnoll; he continued to watch me.

Scooping up the paste, I made my way back over to him. I realised I had made far too much—being toxic in larger quantities, the amount I had made was easily fatal. At least for a human. I put the thought out of my mind and apportioned off a small bit of it, discarding the rest. As I brought it close, the gnoll's muzzle wrinkled at the smell, and he snorted. I imitated putting it in my mouth, and then pointed to his leg. His expression stayed neutral, not leaving my face, and I made the motion again, even taking a small piece of the paste for myself and swallowing it to show him it wasn't poisonous. He held out his hand then, and I wiped the rest onto his palm. Still watching me, his expression unreadable, he then licked his palm clean. I smiled and nodded. I knew it took a little while to take effect, so I decided to sate my curiosity with exploring the shallows by the beach. I did not need to wade far to confirm that food would not be in short supply. Mussels were clumped upon some of the larger rocks near the shore, and fish were evidently plentiful—the water was perfectly clear, and I could see myriad species just from my brief exploration. Hunting would be easy!

I looked back at the gnoll. He had resumed sharpening the spear, but I could tell the nightroot was taking effect. His movements were slowed and clumsy, and the tension in his body spoke of his frustration. I headed back over and he glared at me, whether accusatory or apprehensive, I was unsure. I flinched at that, and motioned that he should set down the both the rock and spear. I pointed to the sticks and grasses I had left nearby, then to his leg. His eyes searched my face, and I could see his nostrils flare—I'm sure he could smell how nervous I was and I hoped he didn't mistake it for betrayal.

He placed both items down, yet I noted they were still well within his reach. He leaned back, placing the heels of his palms behind himself as support, straightening his leg with a wince. I started to place the grass around his knee—a buffer against the hard wood—and then cursed under my breath. I needed something to tie it all together, so apologetically I rose and quickly made my way back into the jungle until I found some suitable vine.

The gnoll was as I left him, although it was apparent the herbs had taken even more of an effect. He looked dizzy, and his arms wavered slightly as he held himself up. I started again, placing the grass around the injured area, then larger leaves to hold it in place, followed finally by the larger sticks. But it was a struggle. I couldn't get the vines tight enough—they'd just snap—and when they were loose the sticks wouldn't stay in position. I tried a number of times, starting from scratch, and there were a few unhappy noises from my patient during the process.

Eventually, I gave up. I couldn't get the splint to work properly and I was frustrated. I looked up at the gnoll, noticing that at some point during the process he must have just laid back and let me tend to him. His eyes were half-lidded and unfocused, and he made soft, whispered, inquisitive noises to himself, looking blindly out towards the ocean. He did not react at all when I prodded his knee, so I took the opportunity to at least confirm that it was properly in joint, feeling around to make sure that the region around the knee wasn't too damaged. Perhaps the splint wouldn't be necessary; at least I hoped so.

I went back to pulp some of the aloe, and slathered some in the wound on his thigh, just above the knee. It was already clean from the seawater, it didn't seem that any sand had gotten into it, and there were no obvious signs of infection—so even though it was rather grisly-looking, I had hope it would heal decently enough. Any fever he had had also seemed to have disappeared. If my memories of nightroot were correct, he would be drifting in and out of sleep for a while, so I decided I'd take that time to learn more about the place we'd discovered.

I left the full waterskin by the gnoll's side and set off down the beach.

The sun had just passed its zenith when I left. The ocean was dawnward, so I decided to make my way starward, with the water on my left and the rainforest on my right. It seemed that the beach generally curved withinwards, enough so that I had already convinced myself we were on an island before I saw the gnoll ahead of me once more. I was quite exhausted at this point; the lack of food for a few days had left me quite weak. Looking up at the sky, the circumnavigation had taken until close to mid-afternoon. A small island, then. And I had seen no signs of any others living upon it.

I wasn't sure how to feel about that. I suppose I had half expected it; my village had known of no lands nearby on the ocean. But it meant we were alone. Not that I wouldn't have been alone otherwise, I thought. After all, the storm had likely left nothing of my home but wreckage, at least from what I could recall of that day. To stave off despondency, I decided to keep myself busy, sitting down near to the gnoll and picking up the half-finished spear and the rock. We needed food, and soon. The gnoll was asleep, which wasn't surprising. At least the nightroot had worked—he hadn't seemed to show much discomfort during my failed splinting attempts, and hadn't even flinched when I tended the wound.

I continued sharpening where the gnoll had left off.

A while passed before I had something I was happy with, and I was eager to try it out, so I waded out into the warm waters to see what I might find. It took me a few tries to become used to the weight of it, but it didn't take long, and soon I had several fish—probably more than needed! I made my way back, catch in hand. The gnoll was awake now, so I waved at him as I approached.

I was ravenous. I didn't bother to clean the fish or make a fire. It had been several days, after all. I sat down next to him and handed him one of the flatfish. He was clearly as hungry as I was, and we ate our meal with gusto. He devoured his frighteningly quickly, so I handed him another.

I caught him watching me surreptitiously as we ate; I put it down to the same curiosity as I felt. Holding up one of the other fish, a mullet, I pointed to it.

"*<Nunum>*," he said. I blinked.

At least that's the closest I can come to representing the word. The way he spoke, the way his muzzle shaped the words, the way it sang deep down in his throat, almost as if he had two voices at once—I could not duplicate it.

"Fish," I suggested. I decided it might do to have some words in common, and I doubted I'd be able to pronounce his language.

"Fiiish," he said. It was close, but not quite right, so I said it again.

"Fish," he said then. In my voice.

I looked at him, shocked, and he laughed—at least I think it was a laugh, though it sounded to me like an odd throaty cackle. "Fish," he said again, mimicking my intonation and pronunciation perfectly, as if another Kunet spoke to me. He continued to chuckle at my confused expression, then seemed to take pity on me. "Fish," he said, more normally, and it was his voice this time. I smiled, relieved. I went through a few more objects—the spear, the stone, and the waterskin—and he repeated them back to me with ease. He offered his own words for the items, too, and I made the attempt; unfortunately, based on his expression and the way his ears swivelled when I tried, it was clear I spoke nowhere near as well in his language as he did in mine.

I guessed gnolls had names, so I tried that next.

"Kunet," I said, patting my chest. I then reached forward and patted his. His short fur covered hard muscle beneath, and I was again reminded at how dangerous a creature he truly was. I shifted away slightly, trying not to make it obvious.

"Kunet!" he stated, confidently.

I shook my head, then pointed to myself. "Kunet," I reiterated, and pointed at him. Understanding brightened his expression, and he placed his hand upon his chest.

"*<Shihma>*," stated the gnoll. Like his other words, the sounds were strange, and it was almost as if some of them harmonised with each other.

"Shima?" I ventured.

"Shima!" he said, happily.

Dreams

*"Dreams show fears more than truth. But there is always
a little of both."*
Tumari Proverb

That first night—well, first real night other than the exhausted sleep upon discovering the island—was a difficult one.

The rest of the afternoon had passed quickly; I taught Shima a few more words, and he seemed quite eager to learn. There were times where I almost forgot we were so different, as we laughed at our shared confusion. Before dusk fell, I went to look for some more fish for dinner; they were so plentiful and I had become accustomed to the spear enough that it posed little difficulty. The ease with which the gnoll and I shared this feast and peppered each other with words and gestures and queries—I think it must have been the euphoria of survival that made me so carelessly giddy. But as I lay there on the beach that night, quite far removed from Shima, looking up at the stars... it all seemed to come crashing down. Subconsciously my hand checked for the knife at my belt, and finding none, I felt in the sand beside me to reaffirm the makeshift spear was still nearby. I was alone, apart from an injured gnoll, on an island I knew nothing about, and I think the natural fears that accompany night's fall removed all of my earlier confidence.

The dreams that night didn't help.

I was back at my village, of course. I was at the beach, helping those on their fishing boats unload their catch. All were heads-down in their work, as was I, but when I glanced up I saw the darkness that was the oncoming storm. I alerted my friends, pointing at the roiling mass in the distance that I knew carried disaster, but they ignored me, waving at me to be quiet, gesturing that I should continue in my work. The *ghaftu* moved closer, faster than I remember, but they were oblivious. They just stood there, bent over, unhurriedly lining up their fish. Soon there were strangely organised strings of fish stretching across the beach, painstakingly ordered by size and shape for what reason I did not know, and still they ignored what was coming. My panicked shouts did no good, so in frustration I turned away and clambered up the bluffs towards the village proper as the dark clouds followed in my wake.

The elders were there, thankfully! I was sure at least they would listen. They were seated in a circle at the village centre, discussing the importances of the day. I could not understand a word of it—it was garbled and unintelligible, as is often the case in dreams—but they each nodded and gesticulated as if it were all not only comprehensible but profound. I yelled at them as the storm grew closer, but it was as if I were not there. I felt something then, against my toes. The swell of the sea was such that the beach was gone, and it was creeping up through the village, lapping at my feet, and slowly rising.

At that, I awoke.

The moon was bright; I guessed it was past midnight. The tide was high enough that the occasional wave was washing over my feet, so groggily I moved higher up the beach. I glanced over to where the gnoll was—he was awake, sitting up and looking my way, and the moonlight glittered in his eyes. His stare unnerved me, and it took me a while to find sleep again.

The sun was already well above the horizon when I woke; I guessed my body was still recovering from the time at sea. The gnoll—Shima—was awake as well, seated in much the same place as I had left him last night, and as I stirred he turned towards me and waved cheerfully. "Kunet!"

I responded with a wave. I stood up and stretched, then walked over to him. "Hungry?" He cocked his head quizzically, and at his blank look, I added "Fish?"

"Fish!" he agreed, and I grabbed the makeshift spear. I was quite quickly becoming adept with its heft and soon had food for us both. I prefer most fish cooked, but I didn't want to worry about a fire; I was still somewhat affected by my disturbing night and was finding it difficult to concentrate. I left two by Shima, both flatfish, which he rapidly started to devour, then sat apart and chewed thoughtfully on the remaining one.

I wondered what had happened to my village. I also wondered why I hadn't really thought about it up to this point—but now, especially after the dream I had, it was in the forefront of my mind. I cursed myself for not having the forethought to drag our raft up further onto the sands. But my village? Did any survive? Had Û or Aea heard their pleas? Was Kana even alive to wonder where I had gone? I couldn't recall seeing anyone when I tried to weather the winds, clutching that large stone. Nor did I remember anyone in the chaos of the ocean before finding the raft.

Well, we could make another raft. There was wood, and vines; there was food and water—well, if it rained, that is. It would take some time, but we could manage it. I realised I included the gnoll in that calculation—but then again, I'd expect he'd want to get back to his village too, if there was anything left of it. I felt I had a basic idea of the direction we had floated, at least.

I looked over at him. He was sitting and watching me curiously, and when I met his gaze he grinned at me—which was still rather disconcerting, what with all the teeth. "Kunet?"

"Shima. Water?"

He nodded, and I went back over and shared the rest of my waterskin with him. He nodded his thanks. "Kunet? Shima spear?"

I thought about that for a moment. It would be a while before he could realistically help me fish, but it would be useful to have another just in case. He started to say something else, in his own language, then shook his head in frustration. He began to hitch himself across the sand closer to the water, dragging his hurt leg, and I could see the effort pained him. I followed him, uncertain whether to try to help, but he soon stopped near where the waves reached their apex and began to draw in the wet sand they left behind. I crouched near him, watching.

First, a simple line—a spear, I assumed. He rubbed that out. He then drew the line again, but had it split into two at the end. "Leg," he stated helpfully, pointing to his injury.

"Ah, a crutch! Crutch," I repeated, at his confused look, and he repeated the word back to me happily. "Water as well," I said, holding up the empty waterskin, and set out to see if any rainwater still remained from the previous day.

Water was simple enough; there was still some in small pools in the more conveniently shaped boulders. The crutch, however, proved to be slightly more difficult. I had no axe or suitable tool I could use for thicker pieces of wood. Most branches I found were either too narrow to support the gnoll's weight, too crooked, too short, too thick, or not possessing the split at one end. I did not mind the search, though. It gave me time to think about what was next, both in terms of getting home, and what to do about Shima. The former, well, there were plenty of supplies in the jungle; I had already decided we could make a raft. Shima, on the other hand, certainly didn't appear to fit the dire warnings the village elders had filled my head with regarding gnolls. He seemed genuinely friendly, and at this point I was happy to give him the benefit of the doubt.

I ended up taking quite a while wandering around the rainforest before I found something remotely passable as a crutch. It rained again, quite hard, while I was searching. I may have been soaked but it did little to dampen my spirits, since the existence of the jungle and regular rainfall suggested we would have no problems finding water. I grabbed a few large leaves and placed them to catch some rainwater, drinking my fill and topping up the waterskin. The exploration had been useful, though. It seemed there were few in the way of dangerous wild animals—the largest I had seen had just been lizards and birds, with the exception of something relatively small and furry that screeched at me angrily from up in the canopy. Fortunately, it was hard to get lost—one convenient aspect of an island, I suppose, since I could just pick a direction and walk until I found a beach. Which is how I ended up getting back, since I had lost any sense of direction under the twilight-dappled green of the forest.

The gnoll had made his way up the beach further away from the water by the time I got back, and seemed quite happy to see me.

His ears were perked forward with barely contained interest, and he quivered with excitement at the sight of the piece of vaguely crutch-shaped wood I bore. As I held it in place for him, he used it as leverage to raise himself up, then managed to get it underneath his arm. It seemed a good height for him and I suddenly realised, seeing him upright, just how tall he was. He was more than a full head height above me, and I was relatively tall for my tribe even though I hadn't gotten my full growth yet.

A flurry of excited gnoll words and sounds washed over me, and at my blank look he finally just exclaimed "Kunet!" He then happily bumped his nose against mine—which I admit frightened me quite a bit—then turned to focus on working with his crutch. It didn't take him long at all to slowly but capably walk around with its aid, and I couldn't help but smile at how thrilled he was with his renewed mobility. Leaving him to his practice, I picked up the spear and went to fish us some dinner.

It took longer than normal, considering Shima insisted on splashing around after me from time to time. But eventually I found us a meal, and we sat together on the wet sand at the edge of the tide and its gentle waves, eating, gesticulating, and drawing, as I tried to teach him some more of my language. I was painfully conscious of our proximity this time; I felt like I was detached, observing myself interact with him. He was so close, and physically dangerous, and yet I was sitting right next to him. If my tribemates could have seen me they'd likely think me a fool. But his every motion, his every expression—they had all seemed genuine and friendly. Finally, as the stars came out and the night grew dark, I excused myself to sleep a number of paces further down the beach. Shima watched me go, but I couldn't discern his expression.

Sleep came slowly, and when it did it was fitful. My mind was restless, and dreams came.

I was in the village again, and the wind whirled around, whipping at my loincloth and tugging at me. The circle of elders was there, still oblivious, even as the seawater lapped at their feet. There were others of my village near me and I grasped at them, but they slipped from my fingers and slowly, ever so slowly, left the ground to join the swirl of winds. It seemed then as if they suddenly realised the danger, and they turned towards me as if to scream for help, but they had no faces and no voices. I grabbed at them, but they were always too high for me to reach. I desperately called to them but didn't know what to say. It was too much and I opened my eyes then; I was lying on my side, cheek resting on the sand, and my heart beat heavily in my chest. I didn't move though, for I heard music.

Shima was sitting on a rock in the shallows. A soft breeze blew, and the waves murmured gently upon the shore. And Shima was singing. He was looking out to sea, but somehow I knew he knew I was awake, whether from a swivel of his ear or the slightest motion of his head, I don't know, but he knew I was listening.

It was beautiful.

I didn't understand a word of it—it was all gnoll—but his voice weaved amongst the words and the breeze and the waves and brought it all together. I swore it sounded at times as if he had more than one voice; there were harmonies there that did not make sense otherwise. It was heartfelt and gentle and complex and intricate, stretching to heights my own voice could not reach and to lows that I imagined I could feel in my bones. I let it envelop me until sleep claimed me.

The world of dreams was not so kind. The sea grew, undulating with the swirl of winds, and I stood amongst the elders as the water rose around us. My ankles, then knees, then thighs; and yet the elders, seated, never noticed even as it rose above their heads. They continued to discuss those things that they deemed so important, ignoring my panicked screams to get them to listen, even as the bubbles ceased from their still-moving mouths. I looked around, and all those the wind had borne away were grasped, one by one, by the rising waves and pulled within. I spluttered as it reached my chin and began to kick desperately to stay above the surface. The swirl of water around me was chaos, and soon I could see nothing but the shadowy forms, only vaguely human, as they were swept away until only I was left. I began to tire, my feet leaden and my legs numb, and then... the raft hoved into view. Painfully aware that I had done this before, I struggled to pull myself up on it, but each time the waves pulled me back. I dimly saw the gnoll's outline atop the raft, refracted through the water as I was pulled under yet again, and I screamed his name.

I awoke, gasping. There was a soft yet solid warmth next to me and I huddled against it, shuddering, as I drifted in and out of panicked sleep. Finally, a calmer sleep claimed me, and I dreamt nothing else that night.

Morning came, and as I slowly gathered together the threads of my consciousness, I realised I was still pressed against something warm and furry. The gnoll was curled up beside me, his back touching my side; this caused me to waken rather more quickly, and I sat up. Shima turned and grinned at me.

"Kunet!"

"Shima?"

He seemed confused at my surprised tone, and his ears flattened slightly. "Kunet no sleep. Kunet hurt. Shima sleep Kunet."

I understood then he had been attempting to comfort me, and I tried to relax. I forced a smile, patted him briefly on the shoulder, and stood. He watched as I grabbed my spear, inquiring "Fish?", and I nodded. I promised myself that I would find suitable firewood today, maybe not for our morning meal, but perhaps later. We shared our meal silently; I think the gnoll was uncertain of my mood, for I kept catching him watching me, ears swivelling, out of the corner of my eye. Occasionally he would sniff the air, as if he could scent my troubles.

We shared a drink, and I spoke. "I think I will explore the island some more."

Shima's bemused expression forced me to add, "Kunet walk."

"Shima walk!" He pointed to his crutch and started to get up, with some difficulty. I helped support him, and he nodded his thanks at me with a grin. When I thought about it, I didn't mind the company. Our exploration might go slowly, but there was no hurry, after all.

Exploration

"There are more paths to take than paws to travel them."
Gnoll Proverb

It was a good day.

We spent its entirety exploring our island. First, we set out to circumnavigate it; Shima appeared quite curious as to its extent, and though I had made the trip before, it was useful to do so without a specific objective in mind. It allowed me to take more note of details, especially since Shima's pace was slower than mine. He also wandered into the shallows frequently, crouching awkwardly with his crutch and peering beneath the waves as they lapped against his legs. His ears perked forward in concentration as he plucked items out, cradling them against his chest as he searched further. After several of these excursions it became clear he thoroughly enjoyed collecting seashells of all sorts and colours, and I wasn't going to stop him. There was no rush, and he certainly seemed happy, which lifted my spirits as well—it chased away the lingering shadows of my dreams from the night before. At one point he exclaimed at a discovery he had made, and spouted an excited flurry of gnollish at me, waving a rock he had found. I approached, and he held it out to me. It was a stone that was glossy and black, and the conchoids on its surface made it immediately recognisable.

"*<Isa'hbnum>*!" Shima stated. I didn't even try and attempt to repeat the word—it held too many sounds I couldn't even begin to make, let alone combine them together.

"Obsidian!" I said, instead.

"Obsidian!" he grinned, and mimicked striking it—knapping, I realised. "Spear!" he pronounced. It went with his other treasures in his right hand—he had been searching with his left, since his right arm was preoccupied with the crutch. We had travelled about a third of the way around the island by the time he became overburdened with his finds; he had difficulty carrying them while also trying to use his crutch, so we paused as he made a cache of seashells near the edge of the rainforest.

The obsidian, he kept.

He was almost childlike in his exploration and excitement. Not that he was a child; I still held to my estimation that he, like me, was young but had recently reached maturity. But there was a genuineness to him that made me smile. He was unafraid of showing his enthusiasm—collecting shells was a thing that gave him joy, and he was unembarrassed by it. He would gleefully show me the ones he found, and it was infectious. So, I found some pretty ones myself, and as I held them out for him to inspect, his open interest made me laugh—not mockingly, far from it, and at his confusion at my sudden outburst I just smiled at him and took his hand, setting the shells I had found amongst his collection. Grinning, he bumped his nose against mine, and this time I did not flinch from it.

About halfway around the island—its duskward side—there was part of the beach and nearby jungle that sloped relatively sharply upwards and inwards. I had noticed it before on my previous excursion, but now I had more opportunity to explore. I had seen the cliff as we approached and figured that this slope might offer a way up. I pointed it out to Shima. He nodded but signalled he would wait; I had noticed he had started to slow with the effort of using the makeshift crutch for such a prolonged time. I'm sure trying to use it on a sandy beach just made it worse. He wandered off towards the ocean to look for more shells while I scrambled up the bluffs.

It did not take me long to reach the top, and I was glad I made the effort for the vantage it provided. The climb had led through the thick jungle growth, but at its summit it cleared, the ground mostly moss-covered stone. The view it provided was a wonderful one. Inland, through some gaps in the trees, I could glimpse the rainforest's canopy spreading out below me. And in the other direction—open ocean bordered by the white sand of the beach stretching out like a crescent, slowly curving out of view behind the forest. Below I could see Shima knee-deep in the water, leaning over to peer for yet more objects of interest beneath the waves. I'm not sure how high up I was, perhaps ten times my height or more. I called out to him, and saw his ears perk as he turned to face upwards.

"Kunet!" He waved at me, and I returned it.

On my way down, I decided to examine the jungle side of the cliff. I was surprised to find a rill crossing my path, and after searching I located a crack high up in the rock face, out of my reach, from which it bubbled forth. It was cold and fresh, and it meant another source for us should the weather not be as kind as it had. I filled up the waterskin and made my way back to Shima.

"Water!" I told him, and handed him the waterskin to drink. His ears perked up, and I motioned that he should keep drinking.

He eyed me as he drained the waterskin, then handed it back curiously. "Wait," I said, and ran off back into the forest, returning swiftly with a newly filled waterskin. His broad, toothy smile reflected my own, and we both finished the waterskin off more than once before we continued. Before we left, I paused. Our landing spot when we reached the island was an arbitrary point; there was nothing to hold us there, so why not make this stretch of beach our home? I tried to convey it to Shima.

"Shima? Kunet sleep here. Shima sleep here. Water. Fish. Home."

He looked briefly puzzled—I had discovered that gnoll faces were very expressive—and I wasn't sure if he entirely understood me, but he nodded. We continued on.

The rest of our trip around was uneventful, apart from Shima collecting further shells of various sizes and shapes. Once Shima recognised our old spot, he pointed it out to me, scanned around for a moment, then, satisfied, he turned and headed back the way we came. I grabbed the spear and sharpening stone that we'd left behind. I let him lead this time, uncertain if there was a specific destination he had in mind. We travelled back to the beach by the cliff and he happily stated "Home!", so I knew he had understood. He was tired, I could tell, and after some cajoling I managed to persuade him to sit and rest. He seemed frustrated that his body was not cooperating—I think he finally acknowledged that the fever had taken a lot from him—so, to mollify him, I quickly collected several mussels bristling from the larger rocks in the shallows nearby, then managed to locate a rather colourful parrotfish that succumbed to my spear, all of which I gave him. He laughed at my bribe but accepted them, and I was forced to suffer another nose-bump.

Leaving him seated there, I made my way into the forest. It was quite a bit rockier than the other side of the island had been, and I found a number of stones that were a good size. I was only able to carry three or four at a time, and as I made my way back over to Shima he watched me curiously, the tail end of the parrotfish hanging from his mouth. I set them down a ways from him.

"Fire?" he asked. I smiled.

"Fire, yes."

He started to stand; I went over to help but he ignored me, focusing on raising himself up unaided. He made his way over to the rocks and started to dig a shallow area for a firepit, setting the stones around the side as he did so. He seemed intent on his work, so I left him to it and went to fetch more. Soon we had a completed firepit, so my next task was firewood. A lot of it was quite wet, and I shrugged apologetically as I set it down nearby. He seemed unfazed, however, and busied himself setting the pit up. By the time I had found brush and small sticks for tinder, he was ready for it, and I handed my load to him. He had already decided on some small pieces of wood for fire starting, and by the certainty of his motions it was clear he was more adept at it than I was. I left him to it and went to hunt more fish.

I was busy splashing around, slightly frustrated that my tiredness had resulted in a few misses, when I heard gnollish exclamations. I turned towards the beach where a proud Shima was waving at me, a broad, open-mouthed grin on his face, tongue lolling, and a small fire burning merrily beside him.

"Shima fire!" he called. I laughed.

Eventually I had enough fish—I had decided I wanted more than the usual, since we had a fire and I thought we were due a celebration. I went and plucked a few large leaves from nearby and set the fish upon them near the fire to cook. I handed Shima a decent knapping stone I had found, which puzzled him, until I said "Obsidian," and gestured accordingly. He grinned and set it next to the chunk of obsidian he had found earlier.

There were plenty of fish for us both, and they tasted wonderful. The orange of sunset joined us for our meal, and by the time we had finished, feeling far too full, the sky was the dark blue of almost night, already scattered with stars. We had been mostly quiet as we ate, as opposed to the flurry of words and questions of the nights before. But it wasn't an awkward quiet. It was, I realised, a companionable silence. We just sat there, across the fire from each other, eating our fish, and the occasional smile or nod of acknowledgement. And that night I think that was all either of us really needed. It had been a good day; my residual fear of Shima had long since dissipated, and even the night felt safer with him there.

Which reminded me of the night before.

"Shima, can you sing? Sing?"

"Sing?"

I paused, embarrassed. I did not have a particularly good singing voice, but I sang a few notes to demonstrate. "Sing," I clarified.

He looked at me. His muzzle dipped slightly, and he glanced off to the side, his ears lowered. I was unfamiliar with gnolls, but I would swear he was blushing. I smiled at the thought.

"Shima! Sing!" I pleaded. He looked back up at me, nervously, then away again. "Come on, I know you can sing, I heard you last night!" I knew he didn't understand me fully, but he could get the gist. "Please?"

I think the tone in my 'please' convinced him; the ear closest to me swivelled, and he looked back over at me. He sighed, and I just sat there expectantly, my eyes on him.

Shima sang. It was tentative at first; he wouldn't look directly at me, but from time to time his eyes flicked in my direction. I was mesmerised. It was like the night before, and his voice felt like it drifted all around us, connecting with the stars, the ocean, the rainforest nearby, in a resonance I could not describe. The words were gnoll words, I could tell, but it did not seem to matter; they still held a richness of meaning to them, and even though I could not put an exact definition to anything, I felt it, and I closed my eyes and let it flow around me.

He stopped far too soon, and the absence of it ached. I opened my eyes and saw him watching me. I smiled at him, and his ear twitched at the emotion in my voice as I thanked him. He looked relieved, grinning in response.

I left the spear near the fire and made my way a short distance away, laying down in the soft sand. I looked over—Shima was watching me from the other side of the fire. He shifted, grabbing his crutch, and started to push himself to his feet. I winced as he momentarily put some weight on his bad leg, and I could see the sharpness of the pain cross his face, but he righted himself and slowly made his way over to me.

"Shima?" I asked.

He lowered himself down gingerly, setting the crutch to one side, then laid next to me, his back pressed against me like the night before. "Kunet sleep. Shima here."

I was thankful for it.

Shelter

"It takes two to make a village."
Tumari Proverb

Days passed, and the moon hid before shyly peeking out once more.

Our choice of the duskward side of the island seemed to be a decent one. There was the source of fresh water close by and certainly no lack of fish. Quite a few rocks in the shallows nearby were encrusted with mussels, and we added those for a bit of variety to our meals. Coconut and cooked breadfruit were occasional supplements, although I needed Shima's help to break open the former. I did occasionally find an herb or two I recognised, as well as some berries—although most of those were poisonous, as Shima quickly informed me.

Shima was certainly adept at making a fire, so I continued to leave that duty to him. I would have just embarrassed myself had I tried, after all. As we spent more time around each other I found that Shima had quite the sense of humour, so I doubt my poor fire-starting skills would have avoided that sort of notice. I could fish, though, and it was something I revelled in. Fish were so plentiful it was hard to fail, and I think it was not so much the challenge that I enjoyed, but rather the gnoll's appreciation that I was getting dinner for us both. His openness and expressiveness were endearing, and I could feel my spirits lift every time he showed joy.

Which often helped. For those first few weeks, rarely would a night pass where I did not have nightmares of my village, but Shima would gently wake me when it occurred. He had taken to sleeping next to me, whether out of a feeling of protection against my dreams, the company, or both, I don't know. But I welcomed it. That initial fear I had of him had disappeared—I knew he was dangerous, but I was convinced now he would never be a danger to me. We were friends, which, even as I realised it, didn't seem so peculiar. Our species had been at odds in the past, perhaps, but I felt ashamed to have so easily painted gnolls with the broad brush I had been given. I had no way of truly knowing whether that animosity was warranted. Was Shima much like other gnolls? Was I much like other humans? I wasn't sure about the former, and I knew I had my own oddities and quirks. I also knew I might never find that answer.

I continued to teach Shima my language, and he picked it up rapidly. Simple names for objects he learned quickly; words for more abstract concepts took a while, probably more due to my inability to suitably describe them in simpler words than his ability to understand them. Ideas like time, direction, and distance were definitely concepts that necessitated a common understanding, but those he quickly deciphered from my crude drawings in the sand. Duskward and dawnward, for example, were straightforward—starward and spearward less so, but it turned out Shima knew of the star that stays still as the rest turn, as well as the prominent spear constellation that lay in the opposite end of the night sky.

Each day we would stroll around our island, sticking mainly to the beach because of the difficulty Shima had with his crutch in the jungle's undergrowth. I would point out things, or try to explain certain words, but much of our time was spent in quiet companionship. He had built up quite a collection of shells, and over the days had relocated his caches to our 'home beach', as it were, which was near the cliff and fire pit.

The lack of splint hadn't seemed to be too much of an issue. The dislocation didn't seem to have been a particularly damaging one, but the depth of the thigh wound did concern me. I frequently helped Shima to apply more aloe, and was impressed at how remarkably quickly he seemed to be healing. When I commented on it he informed me, "Gnolls heal fast!"

I believed it. He was already managing a decent pace with his crutch, and he would put a small amount of weight on his leg from time to time to test it. He asked me one day for a spear—I suppose he felt like he would soon be able to help fish—so I found him a decent spear shaft to work with. We had our 'sharpening stone' near the fire pit, and it took him no time at all to produce a serviceable spear, and I nodded my approval as he showed it to me, grinning.

He spent quite a bit of his time knapping. He was quite skilled at it, which made sense, since I knew the gnoll tribes often used obsidian in their weapons. Together we had found quite a few decent sized pieces of it, and they sat in a small pile near our fire-pit. I decided to watch him for a while one day, and noticed he had discarded the knapping stone I had found for him and replaced it with another. When he saw my confusion, he smiled.

"Kunet find bad stone! Shima find good stone." He grinned.

I sighed. He had an expression that I had come to know well, and I knew what was coming.

"Is okay! Kunet fish," he teased. "Kunet useful!"

I didn't mind. The glitter of amusement in his eyes and the slightest upturn in his muzzle, often along with a twitch of an ear or his tail, told me he meant no harm by it. He liked joking, and I was fine being the butt of it from time to time, though even with my proficiency in the language Shima frustratingly seemed to win the verbal sparring.

Sometimes he would sing. I hungered for those times because it was difficult to coax out of him. He wouldn't say why he didn't sing more often, but I figured it was a lack of words to suitably express it. But he did sing, on occasion. Sometimes, as we walked, he would just begin, and I would do my best to continue to quietly walk beside him, hoping that I wouldn't distract him in any way that might cause him to stop. Sometimes he'd sing at night, when the moon or stars were out. I asked him frequently as we sat together, our meals eaten, watching the vibrant colours of the sunset over the ocean. Sometimes he would, but most times he would look embarrassed, or shrug uncertainly, and I didn't want to press the issue.

Our days were simple and left plenty of time for introspection. I thought about my village a lot, wondering as to the fates of those I had been separated from. It was strange, but they seemed somehow less real now. I could picture them in my mind, especially those I had been closest to, and it would tug at my heart, yet... perhaps the distance made it less? Or the realisation that I might not see them again? Either way, I felt bad for so readily dismissing them, and it gnawed at me. Especially when I thought of Kana.

Shima would notice when it bothered me. Whether my scent betrayed me, or something about my posture, I am unsure, but invariably I'd find him suddenly next to me while I was lost in thought, often realising it only when a cold nose pressed against my ear. Pushing at me with his muzzle seemed to be a gesture of affection, but I was never certain how to respond. I would place my hand on him sometimes, to get his attention, or press closer against his back during the night—he certainly never seemed to mind, at least.

I had wanted to start on a raft for us to return to our respective villages, but decided that a simple shelter would be a more immediately useful task, since it would take much less time and fewer trees. It rained almost every day, not for long, but it could be quite torrential and windy at times, so I felt it might be good for us to have a place to shelter ourselves should a larger storm arise. There was plenty of material—that wouldn't be a problem. Additionally, one of the first items Shima had managed with his obsidian turned out to be a passable axe blade, which, after some trial and error, he managed to affix to a short wooden haft. I mentioned my plan.

"Shima? I was going to build a shelter. For when it storms."

"Shelter?"

"Shelter, like... like small hut," I supplied. 'Hut' was one of the words he had learned, since we shared the concept. Both our villages, or at least from what I knew of gnoll villages, used simple thatch huts.

"Shelter for big rain?"

"Yes, in back of cliff." The leeward side of the cliff, just inside the jungle, provided quite a bit of protection against the weather and would prove a decent location for a shelter. I would need to do some clearing, and it would take some time, especially working by myself. Shima happily pushed the axe my way.

"Axe for cut wood. Shelter!" he explained.

He seemed rather forlorn that he couldn't really help except provide me with a tool, and so I made the effort to frequently take breaks and wander back to the beach to keep him company. Almost every time I made my way back he was waiting for me; I wasn't sure if he heard me approaching or just was lonely enough that he was doing nothing else, and I felt guilty about leaving him alone.

On a few occasions, though, I would make my way back to the beach to find him gone. I'd eventually locate him wandering up or down the beach, collecting various bits of rock, or plants, or the odd flower or two—rather unlike his normal shell collecting he would do on our walks. When I'd ask him about it, he'd inform me he was 'making things', and wouldn't elaborate.

Even then, I think he was bothered by my absence. I caught him several times trying to unsuccessfully navigate through the thick undergrowth to find me, muttering gnoll curses as his crutch kept catching. When he did, we would go for a walk along the beach to look for shells.

One afternoon I lost track of time. I had spent it clearing vegetation in the spot I had chosen, and it wasn't until the light had started to fade that I realised how long I had been working. I felt bad for Shima, so I hurried back.

I found him balancing on his crutch, the spear in his other hand, awkwardly trying to catch fish. A fire was already going in the firepit, and there was a clump of mussels nearby. With a guilty pang I noticed the sun had already set, and the orange in the sky was swiftly fading to a dark blue. Shima grinned broadly when he saw me, excitedly making his way my direction. I met him at the firepit, where he rather disgustedly flung the spear onto the sand, but then he was next to me, ears perked forward, bumping his nose against mine.

"Kunet! Shima make fire, find mussels. How shelter?"

I smiled and told him I was still clearing the area and it would take a while.

"Days?" he asked, tentatively.

"Many days," I explained.

"Okay," he said, but I could tell it wasn't okay. His ears had lowered almost imperceptibly.

Over the time on our island I had figured out a lot of his body language, so even when he tried to hide it I could often tell if things were bothering him. He was generally so unreserved with how he felt about things that it seemed odd when he was subdued. I had come to truly appreciate his company, and I knew it couldn't be easy for him to be isolated, just as it was difficult for me.

So I reached for him and gave him a hug; he seemed a bit surprised, but then hugged me back quite tightly. When I managed to extricate myself, he looked like himself again, so I patted his shoulder and went to pick up the spear, heading down to the water.

He followed me there and watched as I fished. The increasing darkness made it more challenging, but soon I had enough for dinner. I handed them and the spear to Shima at the water's edge, then went for a brief swim to clean off the dirt and sweat from my work earlier. He was still waiting for me, so I accompanied him back to the fire pit. As our meal cooked, he sat quite close to me, and I apologised for having lost track of time and leaving him alone. He nodded and grinned. "Is okay, Kunet! Shelter important."

"Shima important too," I emphasised.

He said nothing, but shifted closer until his side pressed against mine. I noticed, offhand, that the moon was almost full; we had been on the island for about a month, and I conveyed this—with some difficulty—to Shima. Afterwards, we sat there and ate our fish and mussels in silence, listening to the crackle of the fire and the gentle susurrus of the waves. I was quite exhausted—it had been tiring work that afternoon—so I let Shima know and went to lay down nearby on the sand. As was his wont, he laid next to me; we were normally back-to-back, but I felt him shift and turn towards me. His arm cradled me, pulling me closer, and he rested his chin against the top of my head. It was comforting, feeling the warmth of him and smelling his earthy, slightly spicy scent, and I admit it made me feel safe to have him so close. I fell asleep to the sound of his gentle breathing and the soft murmur of the sea.

Starwatching

"One should celebrate all the joys of life."
Gnoll Proverb

The shelter and its surroundings continued to take most of my time over the following days. Progress probably would have been quicker, but I made a point out of not leaving Shima alone for too long, for which he was clearly appreciative. He was still irritated that he couldn't easily make his way back to where I was working, so my first task was to clear a path for us. We'd want one anyway, for easy access to and from the beach, as well as to walk up the side of the cliff to its summit. He helped me with clearing as best he could, starting at the beach and meandering through the overgrowth back to the inland side of the cliff.

Our daily routine started to coalesce. Morning would consist of stoking the fire, catching some fish, refilling the waterskin, breakfast, then just relaxing or walking together. Before the heat of the day we'd start working—I would remove underbrush or chop down smaller trees, and Shima would collect them all into piles. He'd try to help with other things too, but the crutch made it rather difficult for him to balance, so he'd often get frustrated. We'd take a break after a few hours, usually when the daily rains fell, and return to the beach. I'd go for a swim; Shima would splash around in the shallows with his crutch, annoyed he couldn't join me, and

I'd need to make sure I didn't swim for too long otherwise he'd start looking forlorn. Then, after working a bit more, we'd stop in the late afternoon. Fishing, fire, dinner, and chatting filled our evening, and when night fell we'd curl up together in exhausted sleep, his chin pressed against the top of my head and his arm draped over me.

Shima had become more openly affectionate, as well. I think that the day where I had started the clearing process and mistakenly left him alone for so long had made us realise how much we needed each other's company. It was clear how much he liked being around me, and honestly, I felt the same way. It felt right having him close; I didn't mind his muzzle-bumps and hugs throughout the day, and I returned them in kind. We were the only ones on our island and had fast become true friends, and even if objectively it seemed odd to me—a human and a gnoll working together—the peculiarity of it didn't matter.

We made good progress, and after several days had a usable trail from the beach to the section of jungle we'd clear for building our shelter. It was a convenient place with no large trees, making it easier to remove the existing vegetation. An area with a diameter of half a dozen paces or so would be plenty, I figured, to build a large enough shelter to protect both myself and Shima from the more persistent rainstorms.

It was almost fully cleared, and I was focused on chopping away at a particularly bothersome tree with our crude axe, when I realised that I hadn't seen Shima in quite a while. I shouldn't have been concerned, but it was unlike him, so I set down the axe and went to look for him. Approaching the beach from the cleared trail, I caught sight of him walking towards me, grinning. It took a moment for me to notice—he wasn't using his crutch. Although he was limping, he was putting weight on the leg.

"Shima!" I gleefully exclaimed, thrilled to see how much he had healed.

"Kunet!"

I waited until he got close, then poked his shoulder and asked him with a grin, "Where's your crutch?"

His expression was one of exaggerated surprise, but his ears and tail, as usual, gave him away. I didn't mind.

"Oh! Where crutch?" Shima made a show of looking for it, scanning in every direction, even peering behind a nearby tree. "Oh no! Crutch is gone!"

I laughed and gave him a hug, which he returned happily.

"Leg okay. Hurt little. Shima help more!"

He also had some white lines in his fur, clearly something he had painted on. There were three vertical lines on his chest, one on his injured leg, and a line that went from his nose to his forehead. He noticed me eyeing them, so he stared at me and waited for the inevitable question.

"Shima, what are these?"

"Lines!"

"You know what I mean!"

"Lines for… thanking gods? Colours and lines for gods being happy? Shima make sure gods know Shima thank gods."

I nodded. "Is it paint? Where did you get that?"

"Paint?"

"Colours that you put on," I told him.

"Shima make! Come," he said, and beckoned me to follow him back towards the beach.

He led me along the edge of beach and jungle a ways, ears perked with excitement, constantly checking behind to make sure I was following. We soon arrived at some relatively large boulders that he had apparently been using as surfaces upon which to work; there were a number of different rocks, clumps of clay, plants, and other items—I think there were even snails of some sort—separated into groups. He had obviously been using these for various mixtures—crushed powders, sliced roots, ash, and discarded shells were scattered over one of the boulders—but he was pointing to what apparently were the results of his experiments.

"Paints!" Shima exclaimed proudly.

There were several coconut shells which held them. A bone-white, chalky paste in one, a wet yellow-orange powder in another, and a small amount of a vivid purple liquid in a third. I was impressed. I knew of the dyes that my village made but I had no knowledge of their creation, yet clearly Shima knew both their sources and the processes involved. He had certainly been busy while I had been working on the clearing. I had never even seen such a purple.

I glanced over at Shima, who looked quite pleased with himself.

"This purple is wonderful!" I told him. He blushed.

"Shima not find rock for red. Not on island," he explained. He looked rather annoyed at that.

"I'm impressed you found the material to make all you did!"

"Gnolls use paints. Important," he said.

"We do too, but not often."

"Paints in gnoll... important things. What is word?"

"Rituals?"

"Okay, rituals. Yes." Shima put his finger in the whitish paste that he had obviously used in decorating his fur. Before I could stop him, he dragged his white-covered finger down my forehead to my nose. "There! Kunet show gods Kunet happy Shima heal."

"You know I'm very happy to see you feeling better, Shima." I gave him another hug to show it. I had discovered the gnoll was quite tactile, and he greatly appreciated the closeness. I held him for a moment, realising his physical presence comforted me too. He rested his chin on my head.

The rest of the clearing went more quickly with Shima's improved mobility, and he helped me spearfish as the sun crept below the horizon. He revelled in the fact he could finally help me acquire dinner, which mainly consisted of him waving various fish in my face once he had caught them. We had far more than we needed, but I wasn't going to tell him to stop fishing; he was clearly having a great time. Once they were cooked, I picked up the leaf-wrapped package that was the largest one he had caught, and, with a deferential bow, presented it to him. His laughter lifted my heart, and he was chatty long into the night. He even sang, and I was grateful for it.

The next day dawned with an eager Shima waiting to begin on the shelter proper. I assumed just a simple large lean-to would be sufficient, so we set out to collect wood of the appropriate thickness and transport it to the clearing site. I had left two larger trees in the clearing, and got Shima to help me carry a larger log which we'd use as the crosspiece between them. Shima set to work hacking a shallow wedge out of the trees to secure the crosspiece while I collected vines for tying the joints. Soon I needed a break and told Shima so; we had started early in the morning due to his enthusiasm, and it was now the heat of midday.

Shima easily beat me back to the beach, and it wasn't long before there was a loincloth discarded on the sand and a happy gnoll in the ocean. It was readily apparent he had missed the joy of swimming, something he hadn't been able to do while injured, and I sat on a rock in the shallows and watched him play. Without his crutch, he had an enviable athleticism that I couldn't help but admire. I wasn't safe, though; he spotted me, and I was soon dragged out into the water with him. Shima seemed not only full of energy but also quite the fast swimmer, so he wore me out rather quickly. Eventually admitting defeat, I made my way back up onto the beach and laid in the sand, letting the sun dry me off. I was soon joined by a naked gnoll who proceeded to sun himself and wait for his fur to dry.

I couldn't help but look at him. Surreptitiously, of course—I didn't want to make it obvious I was staring. There was a certain level of modesty in my village, and it was rare I saw any of my tribemates completely unclothed; generally, it was just glimpses during bathing or similar activities.

Yet Shima seemed completely unconcerned by his nudity. I admit, I stole glances—I was very curious what gnolls looked like. The pale tawny colour of his chest fur went down to his stomach and continued further; he had a lightly furred sheath, much like an animal, and it hugged low on his belly. He turned to look towards me as I was eyeing him, and face flushed, I quickly averted my gaze.

After a short rest, Shima reclaimed his loincloth and pronounced himself ready to get back to building. I sighed, still rather worn out, but followed in his wake as he headed back.

It took us only two more days to finish our shelter. By early afternoon on that second day, it was all but done—all that was left was tying larger leaves to the sticks that formed the roof such that it would be somewhat dry and rainproof inside, and that didn't take us long. We declared it finished, and Shima hugged me close. I hugged him back.

We had not eaten that day in our excitement to finish our project, so while Shima went to cavort about in the waves, I went to gather food. My haul consisted of breadfruit, a coconut, some turmeric rootstalks, and two types of berries, and after depositing them by the firepit and collecting a few nearby mussels, I grabbed my spear and began to fish. I fetched more than was necessary—after all, a celebration was in order, since it was a milestone of sorts, much like our first fire. He saw me fishing, of course, and came back to shore to collect firewood and build a fire. He was already dry and re-loinclothed by the time I wandered up the beach towards him.

"Many fish!" he pronounced, seeing my catch.

I smiled at him. "Celebrate! Shelter built." It took a few minutes to explain 'celebrate' to him, but he eventually got the gist.

We ate our fill, and given it was still only late afternoon, I had an idea.

"Shima, come with me?" I asked, and held out my hand to him.

He cocked his head at me but took the proffered hand and got up to follow. I led him to the base of the slope that went up the side of the cliff. It was rather difficult terrain and had been inaccessible to Shima when he was using a crutch, but now he was sufficiently healed to manage the scramble with me. We made our way up—Shima had no issue—and at the top I showed him where it opened out from the canopy into the small clearing looking out over the ocean, from where I had waved down to him so many days ago. We sat together on the rocky edge, our legs dangling over the drop, and watched the sun set, its vivid orange setting the distant ocean aflame. Unprompted, Shima began to sing, and it felt like he sang in tune with the sun as it drifted ever downward, then beneath the horizon. I reached over and gave him a hug.

The warm breeze ruffled Shima's fur as we sat.

"Go back to the beach? Or look at stars?" I asked him.

"Stars," he responded, and so we retreated from the ledge to where the rock turned to soft, moss-covered earth near the edge of the jungle, and laid there side by side to watch as the sky turned slowly from blue to blue-black, and finally to black. It was a beautifully clear night and stars covered the heavens. The presence of the gnoll beside me was a tangible comfort; he radiated warmth and solidity, and it took me a few moments to process how important it was to me for him to be there. I pondered how it would have been to be alone on the island, and I became painfully aware how much his constant companionship meant to me.

He had been silent for a while, his side pressed against mine, and impulsively I turned towards him to hug him close. He readily obliged, and I buried my face in his neck fur. I held him tight, suddenly astutely aware of how emotional I was becoming and how

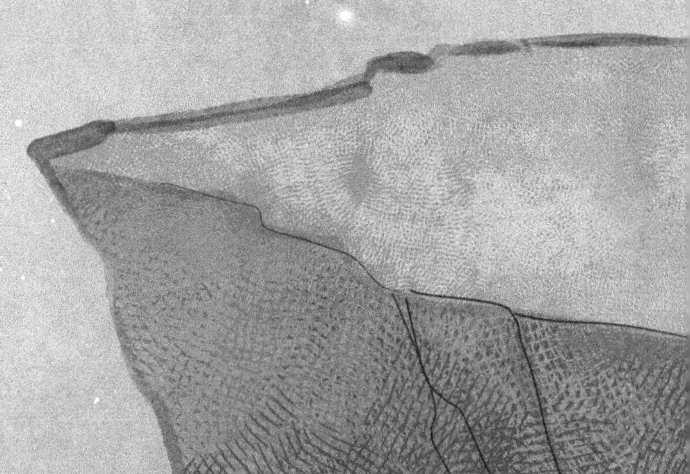

glad I was that I was not alone on this island, but had someone with me. He smelled of ocean and sun and sand and Shima and comfort. He must have sensed something, for he pulled me closer, his arms around me, and nuzzled at me. It threatened to make me cry, so I released him and sat up, trying to calm myself.

Shima sat up too, and I could read the concern on his face, even in the darkness. His worry only served to make me ever more aware of his importance to me, and tears pricked my eyes.

"Kunet?" he asked softly.

"I'm okay, Shima. Really I am. I'm… just glad I'm not alone, that's all."

He said nothing, just watched my face for a time, and I could sense his frustration in trying to find words to help me. Instead, he just reached over and cupped my cheek, his touch ever so gentle.

"Stars still here. Shima too," he added.

I nodded mutely, and lay back down, waiting for the blurriness in my vision to resolve itself into the sharp pinpricks of stars once again.

He laid back down next to me, facing me, and his dark eyes glinted in the starlight. He was silent, just watching me with his ears perked forward, his face mere inches from my own, and I knew he could still sense my discomfort. He started to gently stroke my face and side; his finger pads were leathery and soft. It was a level of affection I had never experienced amongst my agemates in the village, and my throat felt tight.

"Kunet okay?"

The concern in his voice almost made me lose my control. I nodded, and in an effort to not meet his gaze, turned and wriggled closer so I could rest my head beneath his chin. Distractedly, I ran a hand across his chest, feeling the ripple of muscle there. He continued to softly rub my side, and I slowly relaxed, my mind drifting as I played with his fur, enjoying his closeness. I noticed then that his touch was having another effect, and heat flushed my face as I shifted awkwardly, glad that the darkness of night hid me. Unfortunately, now that I had noticed what was happening I couldn't help but be painfully aware of it, which did nothing to lessen the burgeoning arousal beneath my loincloth.

I became minutely conscious of everything then—my breathing, my accelerated heartbeat, my erection—and my mind whirled, panicked, as I imagined that Shima must notice too. His hearing, his sense of smell… I was certain that I must be transparent to him, yet he just continued to gently run his hand over me.

Until he stopped.

He shifted position slightly, and I used the opportunity to roll onto my back away from him. I glanced over to see him on his side, next to me, leaning his head on his hand and meeting my eyes. He said nothing, which was disconcerting. He laid his other hand on my chest, slowly rubbing me; I suppose it was to try and calm me down, but all I could think of was my tenting loincloth in full view.

He stopped again, head slightly cocked, watching me. "Kunet okay?" he asked quietly.

I swallowed and took a shuddering breath to calm myself. I nodded. He met my gaze, and I counted my heavy heartbeats, unable to look away from him. He looked down then, towards my crotch, and embarrassment lit a fire beneath my face. He reached, and with his free hand began to untie my loincloth. My breath hitched as he did so, and he glanced back up at me before resuming his task.

I could barely think, even as it felt the moments stretched. I desperately wanted him to stop, afraid of being revealed. I desperately wanted him to continue, and feel him touch me. And all through it, he continued to unravel the loops that held my loincloth in place.

And then I was naked before him, my erection almost painful, bouncing slightly in time with my heartbeat.

His hand returned to my chest then drifted lower, and I could feel my muscles tense as his fingers brushed my belly, then drift lower once more. I gasped as he started to trace my shape. His touch was feather-light, and he ran a blunt-clawed finger up from my base to the very tip, and I shivered with it. I felt his muzzle press gently against my chin, nuzzling at me, and the heat of his breath on my neck, quicker now, like my own. My mind was spinning, and I don't think I could have moved if I had wanted to, all my nerves and senses eagerly expectant and waiting for his next touch.

He sat up then, and it ached that he withdrew his hand from me. I met his gaze, and I'm sure the need and uncertainty warring within me was writ clear upon my face. His eyes glittered. He was erect too; his loincloth made it obvious.

Shima leaned over me then, and his tongue was hot and wet on my skin, tracing where his hand was only moments ago. It seemed he knew exactly what to do, and slowly and methodically he worked, running his tongue up from the base of my hardness to the very tip. Each time it made me gasp, and with each stroke of his tongue I could feel something building deep within. I watched him as he did so, and his eyes held mine as he continued, pushing me closer, the urgency and tension threatening to break free. Until finally with a cry I spilled forth, splashing across my stomach and chest. I lay there panting, my heart pounding.

He smiled, liquid eyes bright, and leaned forward to lick my cheek.

Then systematically he began to lap up where I had spilled, cleaning me, before returning his attention lower—I was still hard, I don't think it would have been possible for me to not be—and beginning again.

There was nothing else in the world—just myself, Shima, and his soft, insistent tongue. I wanted him so much. Soon the heat of his muzzle surrounded me, and I laced my fingers in his head-fur in a frisson of pleasure. When I finally groaned with release once more, I clutched Shima to me as tightly as I could, and he held me as I drifted off to sleep.

Decisions

"Grasp hold of happiness when you can find it, and do not let go."
Gnoll Proverb

I awoke nestled in Shima's embrace, still naked, and immediately my thoughts returned to the previous night. I wasn't sure how to feel. There was a combination of embarrassment, arousal, uncertainty, excitement, and shame, and all of these were warring within me. I wanted to get up, but I knew that would wake Shima—I could hear his gentle breathing next to my ear. I tried to extricate myself slowly, but he noticed.

"Hello, Kunet!"

He grinned at me, much in the same way he always did, but immediately my mind searched for minute differences, details that might indicate his perception of me had changed or that he thought less of me somehow. Internally I was panicking, and I murmured a muted greeting back to him as I struggled to put my loincloth back on in a manner that didn't look too much like I was rushing. He was watching me, which just made me more nervous. I knew he could sense it too. Even with all my pretence of normalcy, I knew he could scent my consternation.

"Kunet?"

I smiled awkwardly over at him, and suggested breakfast. He nodded and got to his feet, ready to follow me down the slope. He gave me a hug first, which I did my best to return, then nuzzled me, to which I had no real response, so I started heading down. He followed me nimbly, saying nothing. Once we got to the beach, I went to pick up my spear. Looking back, I saw Shima standing a few paces away, looking at me confusedly. His ears were slightly flattened and his tail was dipped.

"Shima? Spearfish with me?"

His expression brightened and his ears perked up. He grabbed his spear and jogged to join me, and it seemed like no time at all before we were sitting at our fire, munching away at breakfast. I realised then I had hunted in silence, and couldn't remember the time between asking him to fish and sitting and eating, I was so preoccupied with my thoughts. Sheepishly I looked up at Shima—he was quiet as well, his muzzle lowered and ears back, looking slightly away from me. I didn't know what to say, for I wasn't sure how I felt.

Since the shelter was complete, we had nothing pressing on our hands. We walked the beach a while and I helped Shima look for shells, but the silence was heavy—it felt like the air presaging the rain before the clouds finally burst. I could feel it, and the more I noticed it, the harder it got for me to break it. When I did speak, it felt forced, even when it wasn't. Shima looked sad, as much as I could discern from gnoll body language, and I was having so much difficulty myself I didn't know what to do to help him.

I wasn't sure I could even place what bothered me so much. Was it because Shima was a gnoll? Was it because his tribe was one my village would do its best to avoid, or at least viewed with considerable wariness? It wasn't that he was male; there were several couples like that back at my village, Paka and Takeh included. Was it somehow representative of me setting aside my tribe and consigning them to only memory? These thoughts jumbled together in my mind, and while inwardly I struggled to make sense of them, outwardly I was silent, and I knew, detachedly, that this hurt my friend.

I looked over, and noticed his ears were still back, muzzle dipped. I opened my mouth to speak, and felt a raindrop, then two.

"Shima? Rain soon, check shelter?"

He nodded and set off for the path into the rainforest, not even looking back to see if I was following. I made my way after him.

The rain turned out to be quite heavy, and there were a number of leaks in our shelter's roof that needed care. We waited it out in silence, and I continued to war with myself. As soon as it started to let up, Shima stood up and went to look for additional material to fix the flaws we had noticed. I followed, helping him to find what was needed, and we set to work.

"Kunet?" he asked, when the silence had become too long to bear.

"Yes, Shima?" I answered.

"Shima do bad?" His ears were flat, and he did not look at me as he asked.

"No! No, Shima."

"Shima gnoll?"

"No... I don't know... Shima," I fumbled, and cursed inwardly. "I'm just trying to figure myself out, that's all. You've done nothing wrong, really. I'm sorry."

He clearly didn't understand what I had said, and it was painful that it was so difficult to explain even with a full grasp of language, let alone when I had to express it more simply. I struggled for a moment, and Shima watched me as I did so. After a few moments, when I said nothing further, he turned and started back towards the beach. I let him go, not knowing what to say, and felt even worse for it.

I sat there by the shelter for a while, sorting through my thoughts, separating them and examining them one by one as best I could. Once I had done so, I returned to the beach. Shima wasn't there; I figured he had left to go look for shells. Or more likely he was upset, I reminded myself. I walked back to the fringes of the forest and returned with some firewood, which I dumped near the pit. When I had tried to set things up for a fire previously, Shima had just rolled his eyes and waved me away so he could do it properly, so I assumed it would be safest just to leave the wood for him. The fishing I could do, though, so I grabbed my spear and wandered the shallows. I decided to slowly make my way down the beach as I did so, hoping to catch a glimpse of my friend, even if I didn't know yet what to say to him.

The sun was low in the sky and I had found more fish than I needed, but had still caught no sight of the gnoll. It was just my luck that I had gone the wrong way, I guessed. I made my way back slowly, checking behind me every so often to make sure I hadn't missed him.

He was by the fire. It was burning brightly; he had evidently been working with it for a while. His back was to me, but one of his ears swivelled my way as he heard me approach.

"Shima... I have fish."

He nodded, and patted the sand next to him where he had collected some large leaves for wrapping the fish while cooking. We sat there quietly, listening to the crackle of the fire. I shifted closer and gave him a hug—he didn't resist, but his return hug was cursory.

"Shima? You're... very important to me. Shima important to Kunet. Shima Kunet's friend. Most important!"

He looked over at me, uncertain. I smiled at him and gave him another squeeze. He grinned at me then, and it was almost his old grin, but it still felt like there was something missing.

We ate our dinner quietly as the sun set.

Afterwards, I went over to the shallows and crouched there, rinsing off my hands. I stayed there for a moment; as dinner's silence had stretched on, I had separated the knotted clump of thoughts in my mind, but I wanted to examine each thread once more before I faced Shima again. I breathed deeply, trying to calm myself—things threatened to fray and jumble and I feared I wouldn't be able to think clearly.

I had never done anything sexual before, but it wasn't that—I'd wanted to, but hadn't had anyone that close to me. It wasn't that Shima was male; I'd always been curious about the other boys my age in the village. Shima was a gnoll, though, and I wondered if my village could ever accept him. Or me for that matter, if we were lovers. I felt somehow I was betraying something unwritten, something that was so obvious and ingrained that it never needed to be stated. But did my village even still exist? I had to stave off those thoughts—there was no point in imagining the worst. What was true was that Shima and I were alone on the island and had only each other. And he had grown dear to me.

I stood and looked back towards the fire. Shima was sitting there, watching me, the flames reflecting in his eyes. I walked over until I was standing next to him, and reached down a hand.

"Shima? Will you watch the stars with me?"

The stars were already out when we got to the top of the cliff, but neither of us minded. They were still there waiting for us, brilliant in the night sky, and the moon had started to show above the trees behind us. So, together we watched the sky turn, sitting on the ledge.

I kept glancing over at Shima. His head was tilted up, gazing up at the stars, but I knew he could tell every time I looked in his direction. His ear would twitch slightly, and I smiled to see how happy he seemed. The relief and joy that had lit his face when I had invited him up here, our place up on the heights of the island, had made my heart lift. It seemed so obvious now, and I admonished myself for taking so long to come to my decision.

I must have been watching him for a long moment, for he glanced over at me.

"Kunet," he said, simply, and leaned over to bump my nose with his muzzle. He held it there, his eyes just inches from mine, so I kissed him on the nose, stood, and beckoned him to join me over on the mossy ground where, only just last night, he had shown me something I had never expected.

Lying there, next to each other, it felt like even the stars were poised, waiting for us. He nuzzled me, pushing his muzzle insistently against my cheek, and I reached over and pulled him closer. I just held him there for a while, delighting in the feel of his fur against my bare skin, his warmth, his scent, his strength, and listening to him breathe against me. His hands slowly stroked me, and eventually they moved lower. I shivered as he brushed against my loincloth, and he grinned at me, extricating himself from my embrace and sitting up. I knew what was next, and parts of me strained for it. He set my loincloth to one side.

"Shima? Wait…" I breathed, and he halted. I looked at him, seeing the flicker of uncertainty on his face, and his ears pulled back.

"No, no, it's okay!" I sat up, and set a hand on his chest, pressing gently, until he had laid back down. I leaned over and kissed him. He looked somewhat mollified, but still confused.

"It's my turn," I smiled at him. I sounded far more confident than I felt; I had no experience in these matters, after all. But I realised there was absolutely nothing else I wanted to do more. So, I slowly untied his loincloth, and set it to the side where mine lay. Kneeling beside him, I ran my eyes over him, obviously curious, since he was a gnoll and I was human. His was… different. I already knew he had a sheath—I had seen him swimming, after all. His testicles were large and tight, and I rested my hand gently on them, feeling their shape. Lightly I trailed my fingers along his sheath—the fur there was the same pale tawny colour as his chest and belly, except very fine and soft. The skin beneath was dark, brownish-black, much like my own, and when I rested my hand there I could feel him start to stiffen within. I slowly stroked his sheath, enjoying the feel of him beneath my hand and smiling at the slight tremors of excitement I could sense in his body. His hardness began to slide forth—it was a deep black, stark against his belly fur. He was soon fully out of his sheath; his was larger than mine, and had a tapered shape towards the end. He gave a little grunt as I started to rub him. I looked over at him then; he was looking directly at me, and I blushed as I continued. It wasn't long before I realised my hand was getting wet—he was leaking—and that just excited me all the more.

The previous night had been almost dreamlike. I had known, obviously, what had happened the night before, but it was difficult for me to fully comprehend, almost like it was another person who had experienced it. But now, with Shima lying before me, and *wanting* me to do what I was doing—well, it all felt like it solidified. Here was someone who yearned to be intimate with me, and eager for me to return it. There was an indefinable feeling associated with that, something I had never had before, that openness and trust and desire all melded together, and that upsurge of emotion suffused me. I wish I could describe it, but I cannot—it is a thing that needs to be experienced. Which I did then, and I treasured it.

He climaxed then with a low moan, and I watched, fascinated, as his seed spilled forth, over his stomach and my hand. I continued to stroke him, slowly and gently, as it spread over his belly. My hand was slippery with it, and I wanted more of him.

I paused then, lifting my hand from him and shifting closer, still kneeling.

My heart was pounding with what was to come, and my own erection was as hard as it had ever been. I felt it brush against his side; Shima's gaze flicked down to it and I felt my face grow hot. I leaned forward, hands braced on the mossy ground on either side of him, and took the tip of his seed-slick spear into my mouth. Dimly, I heard his breathing change, but I barely noticed. The entirety of my focus was on the taste of him, and as I moved my mouth over him I could feel the dribbles of him leaking further, and my own hardness responded in kind.

I moved from his tip and ran my tongue along his shaft, coated with his previous release, which only served to arouse me further. Then back to his tip, as I took him into my mouth. I shivered with the thrill, and shivered once more as I felt him start to stroke my own hardness. I worked him until, panting, he gave me a gasping grunt of warning, and I let him slip from my lips as he started to pulse once more. The sight pushed me over the edge and I felt myself climax from the excitement of it all. I watched as his first few spurts spilled across his chest and belly, then took him again to let the rest spill into my mouth, savouring the male-salt-musk-Shima taste of it.

By the time I had caught my breath again, my arms shaking slightly with post-climax weakness, I let him slip out, the black of his erection still weakly spurting, to rest on the pooled seed on his belly. Shima was panting, jaws parted in a broad grin, his eyes on my face.

"Kunet," he breathed, and he almost sounded shy.

He pulled me into his embrace then, and I buried my head against the fur of his neck and shoulder, his semen slick between our bodies.

I had never been so content.

As I surrendered to sleep I dreamily begged the stars to stay and let the night remain, just as it was. Just for a little longer.

Gods

"Of all the shells in the ocean, a crab will find one that is a perfect fit."
Tumari Proverb

Dawn's light crept through the trees, and I snuggled closer to Shima's warmth. He grunted sleepily, nuzzling me as he held me. I could feel his sheath pressed against my own nakedness, but instead of the embarrassment of the previous morning, this time it just made me want to stay where I was as long as I could. I relaxed against him, and soon his breathing shifted as he drifted to sleep once more. I laid there with him, enjoying his warmth and scent, until finally he awoke. I kissed him, and the brightness in his amber eyes reflected my happiness.

I think that night tore down any remaining barriers or uncertainties between us. In the days that followed, I was readily open with my affections towards Shima. I craved his company, and even though our circumstance may have been brought about by chance, I felt it was more than just being the two of us, alone, with no one else as options. I cared for him deeply, and he responded eagerly to me; it felt almost as if he had been waiting for me to figure things out, things that he had already resolved for himself.

Our days were much the same as they had been—our routine was no different—but there was that extra layer of emotion and attachment that permeated our interactions, and it coloured our days with hues that were much more vibrant. We would walk together, fish, swim, chat, collect shells, and explore the island, and at nights we'd find ourselves atop the cliff, pleasuring each other until we fell asleep. I must admit, the shelter didn't get much use, except for when there was a downpour. The weather was mild, and the joy of being beneath the open sky was too much of a temptation.

My self-consciousness around Shima had disappeared too. I was playful, as was he, and there were many times we'd impulsively start things that previously had been limited to those nights together on the mossy earth.

It was only a few days from that night that I was sitting on a rock in the shallows, my feet dangling in the water, and watching Shima swim. I saw him in a different light now, of course, and it was sometimes difficult for me not to notice his physicality and the ease with which he moved. Even in simple tasks, he had a graceful way about him. And that brought up other thoughts that were hard to ignore.

He popped up, surfacing directly in front of me with that grin of his.

I then noticed the tightness in my loincloth. So did Shima, and he prodded it with a finger.

"What Kunet thinking?"

I just blushed, and in no time he had divested me of my loincloth. I offered no resistance. The heat of his tongue soon made me forget entirely about everything else, and it was not long before I cried out in release. I opened my eyes, panting, to a bemused Shima with my erection in his hand. I stifled a laugh at his expression—apparently I had left a trail of seed all along the top of his muzzle up his forehead. He gave me a mock glare, then dunked himself briefly.

"Kunet paint lines on Shima too!" he grinned, when he resurfaced. I laughed, and he kissed me before diving beneath the waves to continue his search for whichever shells had occupied him previously.

I waited for him on the beach.

He eventually wandered out of the shallows, head tilted down and focused on pushing shells around his palm with a finger, examining them. He shook himself, ridding his fur of most of the water, saw me, and headed my way. I went to meet him, and in response to his quizzical head tilt, I knelt in front of him.

"Kunet?"

"Shima paint Kunet," I told him, smiling, giving his damp sheath a squeeze.

He grinned.

It became a game of sorts between us, a challenge, trying to surprise the other with our rather explicit displays of affection. Shima's playfulness asserted itself quite often, and many a time I found myself having to retrieve my loincloth from wherever he ended up hiding it. We had no really pressing matters to concern ourselves with, in any case. Our shelter was built, should it be needed. Food and water were addressed. And so we were left with time and each other, which made us both perfectly happy.

Over the moons that followed, Shima's grasp of my language increased significantly. There were certain quirks of his that he was strangely steadfast about—he would insist on using our names, rather than 'I' or 'you', for example. He tried to explain it;

it seemed to have something to do with the importance of names and the emphasis on them in gnoll society, and it was difficult for him to let that go.

I tried to learn some of his, too, but my success there was tempered by my inability to make some of the sounds required. He told me that it could still be understood, but the way his ears tilted and flattened at my attempts made me worry that if I met any gnolls, they'd just be insulted at my mangling of their language. But I pushed at it—I felt it was only fair, after all.

It was an interesting tongue, certainly. The way some of the words formed from others was foreign to me, but in many ways they made perfect sense. We were going over parts of the body in gnollish, and many of the joints seems to be named for what they bent: <hhal> was 'leg' and <hhal'kna> was 'knee', while <hma> was 'arm' and <hma'kna> 'elbow'. I know my pronunciation was awful, missing all the resonances that Shima's voice had, and it was

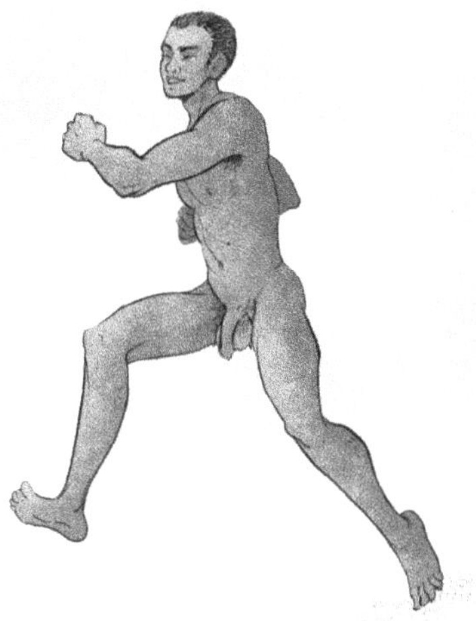

definitely a source of amusement to him rather than a frustration, for which I was thankful. He was overcome with giggles at my attempts at <sraa>, the gnollish word for penis, but he refused to tell me why it was so funny, no matter how much I glared at him. It became an active and distracting lesson shortly thereafter, as I learned that <sraa'a> was 'erection'.

At least with Shima's better understanding of my language, we were able to discuss things we hadn't had the ability to before, and it offered us opportunity to learn more about each other. Some subjects I wasn't sure how to broach, because if it exposed some obvious conflicts between the cultures of his village and my own,

I was afraid it would become an awkwardness between us. But on the other hand, we were very close now. I knew I loved him, and I had no doubt he loved me too.

One evening, as our dinner was cooking and we watched the sun dip beneath the ocean, I was reminded again of my village. There the late afternoon would herald the return of the fishing boats, silhouetted against the suffused salmon of the sky, as the sun itself prepared to depart Aea's domain and enter Û's to give its warmth to her watery world. So I asked something that I had wondered about for a while.

"Shima? Do you miss your village?"

He didn't respond immediately, so I glanced over at him. He shrugged.

"Shima not really miss village. Shima miss gnoll friends."

"What's the difference?"

"Village have other gnolls too," he answered.

"Ah. I'm sorry," I replied, worried that I'd upset him. "There were people I didn't like in my village too."

"Shima is young gnoll. Young gnolls... angry a lot. Many fight. Show who is strongest. Shima strong, but Shima not like fighting."

I could understand that.

"Ayat want young gnolls to fight. If gnolls do not fight, Ayat angry."

I recognised the name from snatches of old stories from the elders in my village. "Ayat—I heard he's the gnoll god. A war god?"

Shima looked at me, intent, and an eyebrow slowly raised. "*The* gnoll god? Gnolls have many gods."

"Oh, I'm sorry, Shima... I didn't mean that gnolls only have a war god or anything!"

He was still staring at me, which, even though he and I were lovers, was still disconcerting. I was afraid I had caused serious offence. He held out a hand and stuck out a thumb. "Ayat just *one* god. Gnolls have other gods too, not just war god! Many different gnoll gods."

I sat quietly, chastised, and waited for Shima to teach me.

"Gnolls also have Sru. He war god." He held up the finger next to his thumb.

"And Uktanu. She war god." He held up another finger.

"Oh, also Rihat. He war god." Another finger.

I gave him a look. I had seen the tell-tale ear twitch—he was teasing. He looked back at me, the picture of seriousness, and nodded sagely. "Gnolls very war-y."

"Warlike," I supplied.

"Gnolls that too," Shima said, straight-faced. He had all five fingers up now. "Anyway. Ettu, he war god—"

"Shima, I know they're not all war gods. I didn't mean it like that!"

"Of course!" he responded. "Other god, Ua, she is—what is word for many gnoll pups?"

"Fertility?" I suggested.

"Yes, okay. Ua fertility god—"

"I knew you were teasing!" I blurted.

"—and war god," Shima deadpanned.

I tackled him, trying to wrestle him to the ground. Soon we were both laughing, covered in sand, and it took quite a bit of bathing and swimming to get all of it out. By the time we returned to the fire our fish was a bit overdone, but it didn't matter. It was still good, and we grinned at each other over our meal.

Shima sang as the sun set. He had been singing regularly now, and it lifted my heart every time he did so. It spoke to me and to the world around me, and I loved it. As we made our way to our favourite place atop the cliff, I apologised to Shima for my earlier assumptions.

"Is okay!" Shima laughed.

"But—"

"Kunet not know. Shima understands!"

He seemed honestly fine, but I still felt ashamed for the broad brush with which I painted his village and their beliefs, the same brush with which I painted his people as a whole before I knew any better. As we lay there next to each other, the stars turning slowly in the sky, I mentioned it again. He shut me up, his muzzle pushed against me, and his lips touched mine. I kissed him back, and then showed him another way I could make it up to him.

Afterwards, as I licked him clean, I decided I wanted more.

"Shima," I said, quietly, and turned so he was behind me. On hands and knees I waited, uncertain how he'd react, my heartbeat heavy in my chest as the moments stretched. I heard the faint rustle as he moved, and then felt his tongue in a place I'd never felt it before. I gasped—it wasn't what I had expected, but I certainly did not mind. As he continued, it only increased how desperately I wanted him, how much I needed him to be even closer than he had been before.

He obliged.

I felt his hands rest on my hips, and I shivered involuntarily as the still slick tip of his erection touched me. And then, ever so gently, he pushed his way in. His shape made it easier, I think, and as he slid ever further I felt stretched and pierced and laid bare all at the same time. He started to move, slowly, back and forth, and I could not prevent the moan that escaped my lips even if I had wanted to. I could think of nothing but the feel of Shima as he moved in and out, and I whimpered and shuddered with it. When he came, he gripped my hips and held himself buried inside me as he gushed forth, and I am certain I cried his name.

He withdrew, and I felt his semen leak out and dribble down me.

"Kunet okay?" he asked quietly, concern in his voice.

"Oh, Shima…" I managed, shaking slightly, shifting to rest on my elbows and lay my forehead on the earth. His hands stroked my back, then lower, and I gasped as his fingers brushed where he had been.

I was sore, even as gentle as he had been. But the absence of him within me ached more; I needed him inside, joined to me again, a part of me.

"Shima," I begged.

He entered me once more. One thing I had learned from our many nights together was that Shima seemed to have no problem continuing once he had spilled. It took longer with each effort, certainly, but I counted that as an advantage, especially then. I craved him, and the night stretched out as I groaned and cried out and pushed back against him, and he responded in kind, thrusting eagerly into me. This new vigour made all coherent thought impossible; my senses were overloaded, and all I could do was gasp and whimper. There was a tightness within me that each push made shudder, and it hurt without hurting as it built and ached and built some more. It swelled and finally crashed through me, and I cried out in agonised pleasure, shaking with release. Dimly I felt Shima's own climax, his heat filling me once again. I remember little else, only the feel of him pressed close to me as we collapsed together to the mossy ground.

Each day dawned with us together, and each sun set the same way.

Over the next moons we started a couple of new projects, the first of which was the raft. We were happy, certainly, but I still wondered what had happened to my village and the people I knew, and I was pretty sure that Shima was also curious about the fate of the friends he had left behind. It gave us something to do, as well. Since the shelter's completion we had had nothing pressing to concern ourselves with, so it felt good to have something to keep ourselves busy.

It was a more precise construction than the shelter had been, and it took quite a while to locate appropriate timber and to prepare and shape it accordingly. Shima was quite knowledgeable about rafts; from my understanding, the gnolls—or at least his village—didn't use catamarans, but used rafts for the times when they needed to go out to sea. Which was rare, according to Shima. There were the main logs, which needed to be large, sturdy, and straight. These would be lashed together with vine, and once that was complete, we would place narrower logs crossways across it, forming a platform of sorts on which we'd ride. Most of our time in those first few moons were spent just finding optimal trees for what we required, cutting them down, and using Shima's axes—he had made another by this point, along with an obsidian knife—to strip off unnecessary branches and shave the logs so they might fit snugly together side by side.

My other project was a more personal one.

There was a type of tree on our island which had bark suitable for my needs, and I spent some time carving out sections of it. The new knife provided quite useful for this, for obsidian, if knapped correctly, can be exceedingly sharp, and since it fit reasonably well in the sheath of the knife I had lost, I had taken to carrying it around. Eventually I had a significant number of sheafs of bark, and I stacked them in the shelter. Shima was curious about them, and asked one day as I sat watching him outline our shelter's clearing with shells that he had collected.

"Kunet? Why many barks?"

"For a journal," I explained. "I figured I'd write on them. With the knife," I added.

"Write what?" He seemed puzzled.

"Well... I'd write of our time here on the island."

"Why?"

"When we finish the raft, and leave? It might be nice to have a record of our lives here," I said.

"Who it for?"

"I guess us?" I responded, uncertainly. "Or whomever we might let read it. But mainly us, I suppose."

"But Shima and Kunet know what happened. Shima and Kunet already made story," Shima insisted.

"Yes, but it's so we don't forget."

He looked at me, and I knew something was coming.

"Kunet forget things a lot?"

"No, I—"

"Hello, Kunet! Shima's name is Shima!" He patted his chest. I glared at him.

"Kunet and Shima on raft. Find island together. Eat fish," he added. "Kunet remember now?"

I sighed. "Of course I remember everything. And I think I always will. Especially you, Shima."

He grinned at that. "Good!"

"I guess part of it is reliving those memories as I write them down," I suggested.

Shima shrugged at that and continued working on his seashell garden. "If Kunet want to write on barks, fine. Shima think it silly though."

"Okay, fine. If you think it's silly, I won't write about you," I said, teasingly.

He looked shocked. "Kunet not want to write about Shima?" he said in disbelief.

I chuckled. "Of course I—"

Shima darted over and swept up the sheafs of bark before I could react.

"If Kunet not write about Shima, Kunet not write!" he stated, and started off with the bark in his arms. Before I could get to him, he had placed them at the junction of a high branch above my reach. He leant against the tree, folded his arms, and looked at me severely.

"I was kidding, Shima. Of course I'll write about you."

"Kunet promise?"

"Of course!"

"Shima worth writing about?"

"You know you are."

His ear twitched. "Good, okay then." He reached up to grab them, then handed them back to me. I gave him a playful shove and started back towards the clearing, then returned to give him a kiss. It seemed to mollify him.

"You know I couldn't write without mentioning you, Shima. What else would I write about, after all?"

"Kunet could write about being short and not reaching barks in tree," he suggested.

"I'm not short!" I protested.

"Kunet short. See?" He walked over and rested his chin on the top of my head. It was something he often did, and I had marked it as one of his many signs of affection.

"Okay, I'll write that. And I'll write that Shima is tall. And big," I added, with a meaningful glance.

Shima grinned and lifted up his loincloth to waggle his sheath at me. "Good!" he pronounced, and squatted back down to place more seashells.

I observed him quietly for a while. I loved to do so, for his athleticism was hard to ignore, and I watched the muscles play beneath his fur. As always, it brought to mind some rather distracting thoughts, so I pushed them from my mind before Shima would scent my reaction and picked up the top sheaf of bark from the stack. Unsheathing the knife, I set to work.

Daylight started to fade, and I looked up, surprised. I had been so preoccupied I hadn't noticed. I had been doing nothing but listing names from my village; I had given little thought to them previously, and I admit I felt bad about that. The exercise of writing their names hadn't helped, for it made me realise how quickly the sharp edges of my memories of them had blunted. It all felt a bit surreal. Faces weren't as clear, even those I had been closest to, and I felt as if on some level I had betrayed them. I wondered how many of those names on the list would have been crossed off by the storm. I'm sure mine had become faded with time in the thoughts of those that had survived. If any had, I thought sadly.

I noticed then that Shima wasn't there. He must have gotten bored with me just sitting and writing; his shell outline for the clearing had been completed, at least. He had also apparently decided to draw an exceedingly suggestive picture near me with his remaining shells. I smiled, rolled my eyes, and went to find him.

Ceremony

The full moon had reached its apex once more, and I went to mark it. There was a large tree near our shelter, and soon after our discovery of the island I had started carving a short slash for each moon's turning. There were thirteen now—we had been here a year. I stared at the markings for a moment; I hadn't known so much time had passed. Shima had been the difference, I supposed. If I had been alone...

Our unhurried construction of the raft was coming along nicely. We finally had enough logs, I thought, to provide the entirety of that bottom layer, and had collected a number of smaller pieces to craft the top upon which we'd sit. We'd bring our spears, and a number of containers for water; several moons ago Shima had helped me gather a few coconuts and break them in half so we had more water containers for when we needed them. I wasn't exactly sure how I felt about leaving, but I felt I should find out what happened to my village. I assumed Shima felt the same way; he hadn't said anything about it, but dutifully worked with me in preparing the raft. I estimated we had perhaps half a moon of preparation left—at our admittedly leisurely pace—before we might be ready to depart.

There was an evening like many others; we sat at the fire together sharing our dinner. Shima sang, as was now happily a common occurrence during our evenings. He had lost none of his ability, and as always, I was entranced. He sang for longer than normal, and kept glancing my way as he did so, which was different. There was a different tone to it too—but as always it was all in gnollish, and though I could pick out a word or two, it was not enough for me to understand. There was an eagerness to it, a focus, as if he wasn't singing to the fire or to the ocean or to the world around us, but as if it were pieces of himself. It almost felt like he was singing to me, specifically, and every time he looked over and met my eyes, he looked almost bashful. It was entirely unlike him.

"Shima?"

I saw his tail twitch.

"Shima, what is it?"

"Kunet! Want to go look at stars?"

It seemed as if he could barely sit still. I smiled. "The sun hasn't even set yet! But if you're that impatient, of course I'm happy to."

He grabbed my hand in his and pulled me to my feet, leading me up the trail to the top of the cliff. I laughed. "Shima, what's gotten into you? We have all night if that's what you want."

About halfway up he lost his patience with my relative slowness, and sped on up ahead of me. I made my way to the top to find him sitting at the cliff edge, legs folded, almost quivering with excitement and doing a rather poor job of staying still.

"Shima?" I chuckled. "What is it?"

He reached out and patted the rock in front of him, bidding me sit. I did so, eyebrow raised, watching him curiously. His eyes glittered, and he waited a few moments just looking at me, a strange expression on his face. My puzzlement only amused him, and he grinned widely.

"Kunet!" he pronounced, and pulled something from behind his back. Detachedly, I determined he must have left it at the top of the cliff earlier, because I didn't see him carrying anything on the way up. It was one of the prettiest shells I had ever seen—it was large and spiralled, and the pale pink of its interior glistened with an opalescent sheen. Unfortunately, it wasn't whole; it looked like its time amongst the waves and the rocks had broken it. But that which remained was truly beautiful. Shima had apparently taken the time to somehow put a hole in it and string it on a vine, like an amulet. He scooted closer to me and placed the amulet over my head. The shell had a nice weight to it, and bounced lightly against my chest.

"Ah, Shima... it's wonderful! Thank—"

He interrupted me with a clawed finger pressed against my lips. His grin was back, and he reached behind himself to pull out something else. It was the shell's twin—the missing piece. It was also threaded with a piece of vine, and he gently took my hands, pulling them towards him and tilting my palms upwards. He laid the amulet in them. I looked up at him—he was waiting expectantly.

So, I reached up. He was a bit too tall, and he chuckled as he bent his head down to receive the necklace. He took the shell in his hand then, and leaned forward for mine. Of course, they fit perfectly—I had had no doubt—and he sat back, clearly pleased.

"Shima find these. A thing, broken. But together, one beautiful thing! Two pieces that go together. Like... clamshell, with two pieces that close. If only one piece, clam not work very well. Or like, like…"

He reached over to take the knife from my belt.

"Like knife and sheath—things that go together." He pulled the knife out of the sheath and pushed it back in to demonstrate. I saw an ear twitch. He looked up at me then, and suggestively pushed the knife in and out of the sheath multiple times, leering at me. I rolled my eyes, and he gave me the knife back.

"Or… like sunrise and sunset. Things that go together," he stated and paused, meeting my eyes intently. "Like Kunet and Shima," he continued, leaning forward to bump his nose against mine.

"Kunet and Shima go together. Broken things apart, but when together, beautiful thing." He looked embarrassed, and his ears went back as he looked down and to the side. "Is gnoll thing, gnoll… what is word? Special happening?"

"Ceremony?" I suggested softly, trying to keep my voice from breaking.

"Yes! Gnoll ceremony. Because Kunet and Shima one beautiful thing. Let Shima remember words…"

He seemed perked up again and deep in thought, and after a moment he started murmuring, almost sing-song, and I could tell it was his own language—it sounded similar to the words in the songs he would sing. I could tell the power and emotion of it. His voice was shaking, and he trailed off, his ears going flat again.

"Shima loves Kunet," he said, simply. He looked at me. "Kunet! Don't cry, Shima is sorry Shima can't remember ceremony words."

"No, no! Shima, I'm not crying from that. I am happy. Kunet loves Shima too. And it's fine if you don't remember any of the words! Is there... is there something I'm supposed to do for this ceremony?"

Shima seemed satisfied I wasn't upset and shrugged uncertainly. "Say certain gnoll words back, but Shima not remember them. Shima sorry!"

"It doesn't matter, Shima. The words aren't important." I kissed him gently, my mouth lingering on his. "Will that work instead?"

"Yes," he grinned. He looked relieved, as if he thought I wouldn't accept his offer. I reached forward and pulled him toward me, hugging him tightly. He held me for several moments, then released me, holding me at arm's length. He just stared at me, and I could tell there were emotions within him just pushing to escape. There were for me too. He reached up with a thumb to wipe one of my tears away.

Eventually I broke the silence. "Shima? Is there more to this ceremony?"

Shima's reverie was broken, and he grinned. "Yes! Dance."

"What?"

"Dance! Move body around? Happy thing? Shima not get word right?"

I laughed. "No, that's right. Wh—"

My question was interrupted as Shima yanked me to my feet and started to lead me back down along the path towards the beach.

"I'm not sure I know the right dances, Shima," I managed, as we scrambled down.

"It not matter! Dance is happiness, not matter which dance. First paints though," he added.

I followed him to the rocks where he kept his pigments. They were very much Shima's thing, so I would not interrupt him when he decided he wanted to work on them, which happened on occasion—usually when I was busy with my 'barks'. But he had clearly done some recent mixing; all three of the colours he had managed to concoct in the past were freshly made. His ears flattened somewhat, and I looked up at him, concerned.

"Shima still not find rock for red paint."

"It's okay, Shima!"

"Red part of ceremony though."

"Well... you said the dance does not matter, but it is the happiness, yes? Can't it be the same with the paints? The intent is there, even if the colour is not?"

He thought about that, and finally nodded his assent. "Kunet is right. Colour not as important." He stuck a finger in the white paste and squatted on his haunches in front of me so his eyes were level with mine. After a quick nose-bump, he started to draw on me—my arms, my chest, my stomach, even a couple lines on my face. Then he switched colours and painted more. Soon, I had various designs all over my body, in white, yellow, and purple, and Shima eyed me critically.

"Kunet look good!"

I wasn't going to argue, but watched with some amusement as Shima attempted to paint similar designs on himself, his tongue sticking out the side of his muzzle in concentration. I ended up helping him on some of it, and he was very particular that I get the shapes right. He eventually pronounced it good enough, and grinned at me.

"Take loincloth off now!"

"What?" I asked. Shima was already divesting himself of his own.

"Dance naked!"

I crossed my arms and gave him a look. "Are you sure this isn't an excuse to have me naked?"

Shima gave me a patient look. "Shima not need excuse for that," he smiled. I blushed and obliged.

"Anyway. In village, rest of tribe dance too. Two who fit together dance naked," he continued.

"In front of everyone?"

Shima looked puzzled. "Yes? Is ceremony. No rest of tribe here though," he said, sadly.

It was often difficult for me to tell how much he missed his village; I know I missed mine, but having Shima with me pushed it to the back of my mind where it sat, hidden, until some random occurrence, even something as simple as the way the sunlight might reflect off the water, would push it to the forefront. And I would wonder, again, how my fellows had fared. I looked over at Shima—his muzzle was dipped and he seemed lost in thought. I took his hand.

"The stars can watch us, Shima," I smiled. "Show me how to dance."

And he did.

There, on the sand, as one by one the stars began to prickle the darkening sky, we danced. At first I performed the dances I knew, the ones from my village and our celebrations. Through it all I was watching Shima as he moved—as always, he had a grace to him that I could not duplicate. After a time I broke off, pausing for breath, and simply observed him; there was a design to his dancing, a rhythm underlying, but it seemed like none of his motions were repeated exactly. He eventually noticed me eyeing him and stopped, tongue lolling.

"Kunet?"

"What is that dance?" I asked him.

He shrugged. "Is dance that is dance for now."

My confusion must have been plain, for he continued.

"Is dance that Shima makes from Shima joy with Kunet. Shima and Kunet make song, and Shima is singing with dance," he said, and his ears flattened slightly at my perplexed look. "Shima will sing too with voice?" he offered.

"I would love that," I smiled. He grinned in return and began to dance once more, but this time he was watching me throughout, meeting my gaze. Then he started to sing, his face intent on mine as he moved, and the song somehow matched the dance—not rhythmically, or in any typical way, but rather the feel of it, the way his songs had a way of weaving amongst the world around him. And his dance reflected that as well.

He paused. "Kunet try too!"

"I... don't know how, Shima," I said, and my self-consciousness and anxiety started to take hold. He must have heard it in my voice, because he grabbed my hands and pulled me to stand next to him.

"Is easy! Just... listen to Shima voice. Song has feel, and make dance say same thing."

I tried. It was difficult to let go and just feel things the way Shima suggested, but as he sang, I felt hints of how a dance might match. They were just glimmers—like the brief flash of sunlight off an obsidian speartip, or seeing something out of the corner of one's eye—but I could not hold onto them. But in those ever

so brief snatches of feeling, I knew what he meant. He noticed, somehow, and encouraged me, and I felt that swell of accomplishment as I reflected pieces of his song, even though they were but eyeblinks in the expanse of his music.

The sky was blue-black now, and sprayed with stars. I was tired, both from the physical exertion and the strain of reaching for things I could not quite grasp. Shima, as always, was very aware of how I felt, and he let his song die off. He moved close to me, embracing me gently, and wordlessly led me out into the ocean so we could wash the paint off each other.

There is nothing more that I wanted other than to be close to him at that moment.

"Shima," I whispered in his ear, and it twitched. "Let's watch the stars, and I'll show you how important you are. Together we can be a beautiful thing."

He was only too eager to oblige, so we made our way up the cliffside, and soon we lay together upon the moss like we had so many times before. In no time at all his tongue found me, and his own desperation and need was on ample display, hanging heavy and swollen and black from his sheath. I knew what he wanted most, so I turned for him, and his tongue found new places. It was only moments, and then I could feel the strength and warmth of him against my back as he pressed against me, his breath hot near my ear.

I moaned his name as he entered me.

Having his heat stretch and fill me made me complete. There were no times when I felt as much a part of Shima as when he was inside me; all my world was focused and pinpointed on the two of us together—there was nothing else. I would shudder and whimper, incoherent with the emotion and need of it, and as he came and pulsed deep within me, I could think of nothing else but him.

That night he reached his climax quickly, but it was by no means over. He continued twice more, his ecstasy and mine melting together. My limbs felt shaky when he withdrew, but he wouldn't let me rest; he was insistent I take a turn too. He laid on his belly, his tail shifted and upraised, and I mounted him. He emitted little growls with each thrust I made; I could feel them vibrate along my length, and it was not long at all before I groaned in release. My semen had made him slippery, so I began again, harder this time, and the noises he made pushed me to redouble my efforts. I made him mine once more, leaving my seed, and he whispered my name.

Something from our makeshift ceremony of earlier made all of it that much more intense. There was an acceptance of each other as our other half, a final barrier broken, and our lovemaking reflected it. Though I pulled out, physically spent, it had not dampened my craving for him. I lay on my back on the soft moss, the cool breeze welcome, and Shima shifted to brace himself above me, his hands on the ground on either side of my shoulders. He grinned, leaning down to kiss me.

"Kunet felt good," he said. I blushed.

"So did Shima," I replied. I looked down, and the seed-wet blackness of his erection hovered between us. I started to turn over for him, but he stopped me with another kiss.

"Kunet stay on back," he said. "Shima wants to see Kunet's face."

He knelt and bade me lift my knees, and soon he was pressed against me, his thighs against my rear, his spear proud and resting upon my reawakening arousal. A slight shift, and he slipped easily into me. Slowly and gently he made love to me, his eyes on my face as did so, and I pulled his head lower so I could kiss him. He made me his, and I surrendered to him.

Gnolls were more than capable, as I had experienced before, and even as the flow of his heat filled me, he continued. Several more times he emptied inside me—I lost track, for coherent thought was impossible. There was something about his position and the angle of him, and I know I spilled upon myself at one point as he pushed against me. By the time he was done and laid by my side, I could do little else but wriggle closer to him; he pressed as close as he could to me, his chest to my back. I felt him slip inside once more, to be together as one as much as we possibly could, and we fell asleep with him deep within me.

Dawn had passed us by when we awoke. I was still entwined with him, although he must have slipped out of me as we slept. There was a blissful ache within me from Shima's vigour the night before—I felt I'd have trouble walking, so I just wriggled around in his embrace so I could face him. His dark amber eyes were inches from my own, and I kissed him on the nose, prompting the grin I had grown to love so much. I buried my head in the fur of his neck and just laid with him a while, listening to the morning song of the nearby jungle.

"Shima?" I asked, as I absently played with his sheath. He responded with a sleepy questioning grunt.

"What will the villages think?" I wondered. "I mean, once we go back."

"What Kunet mean?"

"Well, I don't know how my village would react if I just show up with you."

"Is okay. Kunet gnoll now, go to Shima's village," Shima said matter-of-factly.

"I don't think they'd see me as a gnoll," I replied doubtfully.

"That not matter. Kunet not look like gnoll. But Shima and Kunet do ceremony. Shima loves Kunet, and Shima and Kunet are one thing now. So, gnolls accept Kunet," Shima stated, as if it were the most obvious thing in the world.

I wasn't entirely convinced, but I didn't care. Shima was next to me, and that's what mattered. Soon he was closer; my insistent touching had resulted in an insistent gnoll, and even though I was sore I welcomed him, as he made me his once more.

Divination

"No one truly knows the will of the gods."
Gnoll Proverb

The raft was on my mind almost constantly. Not the building of it, for that was straightforward and going smoothly, albeit slowly. It was the questions it raised that occupied me. Would my village be there? Would my tribemates? What about Shima's tribe? Would we even be able to find our villages? And if we did, what would happen with the two of us? I think this was the question that bothered me most of all, for I had no idea how my own tribe would react to me having a gnoll for a mate, let alone if I'd be accepted in Shima's. And even as I would sort through and manage to momentarily discard one of these worries, another one would push its way to the forefront.

It was impossible to hide my anxiety from Shima, of course. A flare of his nostrils as I approached and he'd know my emotions as well as I knew them myself. I tried expressing the things that bothered me and Shima would listen attentively, but he seemed unconcerned, thinking they were less an issue than I was making them out to be. I wished I had his confidence that things would just work.

He did his best to help me forget my worries. At night, when he had me encircled in his arms, I was able to just think of Shima. At other times, Shima being Shima, he'd also use more direct methods of distracting me, which I didn't mind.

We had just finished our lovemaking and I was lying on my side, pressed close against him. He was still inside me, and I sleepily shifted closer; I had quickly grown to love falling asleep when we were still joined together. I was drifting off when I felt his finger trace my cheek. I tilted my head to look up at him; he was propped up on his elbow, looking down at me.

"Kunet trying to become gnoll now?"

"What?" I asked, blearily.

"Is okay. Gnolls better thing to be anyway." He continued to run his finger along my cheek.

"What do you mean, Shima?"

"Well, Kunet trying to grow fur now. Little fur, almost not there." He rubbed my cheek, and his leathery finger pads made a raspy sound against the faint growth of fuzz there.

I chuckled. "I need to cut my hair again, too. It's getting too long!"

"Is okay though. Kunet not need fur to be gnoll. Village will accept," Shima insisted, knowing it was one of my many concerns.

"I don't know anymore, Shima. I don't know what to expect, or what to do," I murmured quietly—I was tired, worn out from Shima's earlier attentions.

"Can't know. Well, maybe gods know. But will be okay, Kunet." He laid his head back down on the moss, his chin resting against the top of my head, and pulled me to him, making sure I was as close as possible.

Maybe the gods did know. I wondered if I could ask them.

It was morning, and I was sitting on the beach while Shima amused himself looking for shells. I had the obsidian knife out, and was doing my best to cut my hair while it was still wet from the sea. In my village, the men tended to be clean-shaven and keep their hair very short—it was a tradition I had continued since we arrived at the island. The breeze off the ocean picked up the discarded curls and blew them away as quickly as I cut them.

Shaving, however, proved far more awkward.

I understood the theory, of course. But after a few nicks and cuts—the obsidian was very sharp—I became frustrated. Which produced yet more cuts. My curses must have been picked up by Shima's sensitive ears, because before I finished I saw him walking towards me along the shore.

"Kunet?"

"Hello, Shima," I managed, through gritted teeth.

"What happened? Blood and cuts on Kunet's face."

"I'm trying to shave." I half-heartedly waved the knife in the air as evidence.

There was a long pause, and I closed my eyes, waiting for him to express his amusement as I knew he would.

"Did Kunet lose?"

"No, I'm just... not very good at it," I admitted.

There was another pause.

"Is good Kunet not use axe."

Exasperated, I opened my eyes to glare at him. He was grinning, of course.

"Is okay. Shima can help." He sat himself down facing me, legs crossed, and held out a hand for the knife. Sighing, defeated, I handed it to him.

I admit, Shima did far better than I did. He nicked me once, and when I winced his ears went all the way flat against his head. I had to tell him everything was okay several times before he would continue, and when he finished I kissed him on the nose.

"Thank you, Shima."

"Shima will cut Kunet's fur next time, okay?"

I happily agreed, and I accompanied him back to the shallows to help him in his search for seashells. Ostensibly, at least—I was actually looking for stones.

Back at my village, one or two of the elders had performed divinations with stones. They would toss the stones, and said the gods spoke through them in the way they fell. Mainly Û, from what I recalled—she was very much a god on whom our prosperity depended. The elders would collect the stones in the shallows, since if they were chosen from her domain, she might deign to offer answers. I remember watching, as a child. I was entranced; the stones fell, scattered about in a pattern that made no sense to my eyes, but the shaman would speak of each stone and why it was there, and why it was close to certain other stones, and it would all come together and seem so simple.

It couldn't hurt to try.

I remembered the stones being very recognisable, so I was searching for appropriately distinctive specimens. The hard part was figuring out exactly what they should represent. I found a lovely green one, tumbled smooth by its years in the waves, and decided that would be Shima. A slightly smaller dark one for myself, and a squarish flat one for the raft. It was hard to find aspects in the rocks that could meaningfully depict all the things I wanted in my divination, so I ended up settling for uniquely coloured and shaped rocks, or at least different enough I'd have an easy time telling them apart. In the end, I also found stones for both my village and Shima's, the ocean, the moon and sun (I remembered these from the elder's collection), gnolls, and humans.

"Those strange shells," Shima noted, as he saw me carrying my collection up onto the beach. He followed. "What Kunet doing?"

"I'm going to try a divination," I explained.

"What?"

"I'm going to try and ask the gods if they have any advice or blessings for us, for our journey."

"With rocks?"

I told Shima what I remembered from the elders in my village. He listened, saying nothing, but followed me as I went to sit in the damp sand near the push of the tide. He sat across from me, watching curiously. I cupped my hands together, the stones within, and they clattered against one another as I shook them. Silently, I thought of what I wished to know, and hoped the gods would hear.

The sand lay there between us, a blank slate, and I tossed the stones down.

I stared at them a while, trying to make sense of it. The silence was too much for Shima.

"Looks like rocks," he said, helpfully.

I sighed. "These are supposed to represent things, but I don't see how they connect."

"Which one is Shima?"

I pointed. "The green one."

He tilted his head at me. "Why is Shima green?"

"Because it was the prettiest stone I could find. And you are pretty," I smiled at him.

He grinned back, and was quiet, briefly.

"Which one is Kunet?"

I pointed at it.

"Why so far from Shima? That's not right." He sounded worried, and picked up the green one and set it next to the Kunet-stone. "There!"

"No, Shima, it's—"

I gathered them up and waited for the sea to flatten the sand again.

"—it's intended to be something we just look at. It's supposed to help tell us what the gods think." I tossed them again.

He waited, while I stared at the configuration there on the sand.

"Still looks like rocks," he offered.

"This seemed so straightforward when our shaman did it. He looked at them and spoke about them and it all made sense!" I was getting more frustrated by the moment, and it joined the anger I held for what the gods had allowed to happen to my village. "Perhaps the gods aren't listening."

"Why gods use rocks?"

"What?" I said, distracted briefly from my annoyance.

"Why gods use rocks? If gods want to speak, gods should say things. Rocks confusing, not know what rocks mean."

"Did your gods speak to you?" I asked, intrigued.

"No, Shima not have rocks," he grinned. I glared at him.

"Gods speak to...*<kishpsibi>* sometimes, maybe? Not speak to Shima," he continued. "*<Kishpsibi>* like...gnoll shaman."

Dejected, I gathered the stones up and hurled them back into the shallows. Shima's ears flattened at this, which made me feel worse, so I apologised and set off. I would find some firewood—something that I could easily be angry at, other than gods.

I was gone longer than I had intended.

I don't know why my failure at stone reading bothered me so much, and I didn't have the mindset to sort through it. I was angry. Angry at the stones, angry at the gods for not answering, angry at the gods for being aloof and detached and uncaring and destroying my village, and most of all angry at myself for possibly upsetting Shima. So I took my aggression out on firewood, and managed to collect—and break—quite a bit of it before I had calmed down.

Looking back on it, I think it was my fear of what was to come, when our raft was complete.

I didn't see Shima again until I made my way back to the beach. He had started a fire, and waved at me when he saw me with my load of firewood. I dumped it nearby and went to give him a hug. "I'm sorry, Shima, I'm just worried," I explained, sheepishly. He held me for several long moments before letting me go.

"Is okay! Shima found crabs, guava, also breadfruit. Oh, and bird!" Shima informed me happily, holding up a mostly-plucked seabird of some sort.

I stared at him. "Where did you get a bird?"

"Oh, Shima make bird noise." He demonstrated—it sounded exactly like the ones I'd seen occasionally roosting in the coconut trees near the beach. "Birds think Shima is bird, get too close, Shima throw rock. Birds not smart."

Later, after a tastily different dinner, when I carried the axe back to its place in our shelter, I discovered he had found something else too. Sitting on the sheafs of bark were two stones placed next to each other, a vivid green one and a smaller dark one.

Raft

"There are choices in life that make all the difference."
Gnoll Proverb

By the next moon, the raft was on the verge of completion.

We had dragged all the logs out onto the beach, ready to be bound together with vine as best we could. They had already been worked so they fit snugly, but even so it took us most of the morning to attach them securely. After that it was the cross pieces, which proved a bit more involved than we had expected. But as the sun set, we looked upon our finished raft. We had worked in silence for most of the day; I know I had been alone with my thoughts, and I presumed Shima had been too—though it hadn't prevented him from playfully trying to tie my leg to one of the logs.

As we fished for our dinner, I still felt that weight. Concern for what was to come, anxiety about going out to sea once more, and what if our villages were no longer? Shima had seemed unfazed by the prospect of meeting our respective tribemates, but I was still quite nervous. Whenever he caught me looking over at him, he gave me that warm grin of his, and I wondered if I was the only one with these worries. Shima seemed fine.

We ate, sitting side by side, and I could focus on nothing else but the fact this would be our last night on the island. I didn't know how to feel. Shima could sense my turmoil—he always could—and snuggled closer, pulling me so I was sitting with my back against his chest. He had already finished eating, and he rested his chin on the top of my head, his arms around me, while I picked at the remainder of my food before setting it aside in frustration.

Shima started to sing. It was less a song as most of his other tunes—it seemed directionless—but it was slow and calming. The low notes thrummed through me; I could feel them vibrate where I was pressed against his body. It was familiar, and I realised it was similar to the singing he had done when I had had those night-mares, so long ago now. I relaxed, and eventually he let the notes trail off to merge with the whisper of the waves.

We made our way up to our vantage point on the cliff and made love slowly, long into the night. Afterwards, with Shima pressed against me and snoring softly, I laid awake and watched the stars slowly turn. I watched Shima too—his face was relaxed and content, and I wished I could be as unworried. It was a long time before I found sleep.

That morning we lingered, lazily, and took our time fishing and eating, followed by a final circumnavigation of our island. Shima said little, as did I. It wasn't until afternoon that we collected the various belongings we'd take along. There was the knife and waterskin, of course, along with several coconut halves we had acquired over the past year as extra water bowls for catching the rain. There was an oar that Shima had shaped with the axe; we knew our villages likely lay dawnward, but little more than that. We'd take the spears as well, along with the axe and the sheafs of bark I had thus far written. As was his wont, Shima poked fun at them again, deciding to carefully pronounce various words for me to make sure I hadn't forgotten. "Spear! Raft! Shima!"

But before we'd load up to go, we would check seaworthiness.

The raft was extremely heavy, and I soon wished we had built it slightly closer to the water. It was mostly Shima that managed to get it the rest of the way—I felt like I was little help. Together we pulled it until the waves held it up, then pushed it further out until we were hip-deep. Sitting atop it didn't submerge it, so we pronounced it good to go.

It was a perfect day, cloudless and blue. All we needed was to fetch our things from shore, but before we did, I looked over at Shima. He was watching me, his amber eyes locked on mine, expressionless. We stood there in the ocean for several long moments, our hands on the edge of the raft, holding it still as the waves gently bucked it. Something unspoken passed between us then, and together we waded deeper, pushing the raft before us.

And let it go.

We watched it as it slowly receded into the distance. I stepped closer to Shima and he put an arm around me, and we waited there until it was barely a speck on the horizon. It was meant for that other world, after all. Not ours. Our world was the island and each other. We needed nothing more.

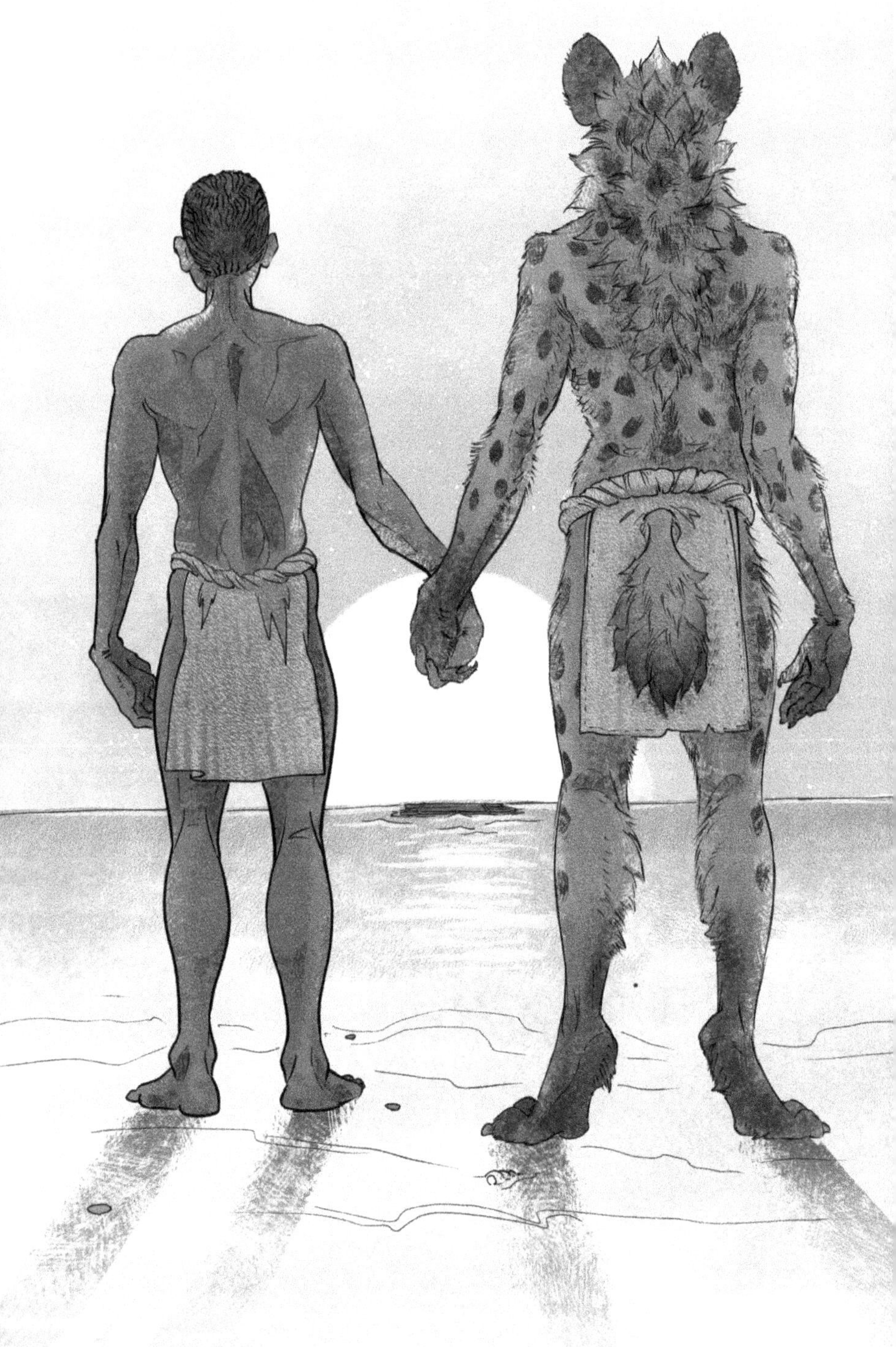

Years

"Beware, for there is always danger."
Gnoll Proverb

With that last vestige of our connection to the outside world gone, I think we were truly content. It was just us now, and it always would be. The years stretched out ahead of us, laden with possibility, and we knew we'd share them here, with each other. Both Shima and I knew the truth of this in our hearts, and though we said nothing of it that day after the raft floated into the distance, the way we held each other tight that evening made it clear we both happily accepted it. That raft had been a link, a tenuous thread that held us to the world we'd left behind, and it had fallen heavier on us than either of us realised. But now it was gone, and the weight was lifted.

Our true home, the island, beckoned us now.

Those next days we spent doing absolutely nothing of import. We simply wandered the island together, collecting shells, swimming, chatting. Making love on occasion when the mood took us, right there on the beach. And of course, joining with each other much more extensively as the stars spun against the blackness of the sky.

Days turned, the moon turned. Days to moons, and moons, eventually, to years.

I kept track, as I had done, slicing marks onto the tree. There was no real need to denote the passage of time other than, I suppose, curiosity. I also used it as an excuse for anniversaries of sorts: the arrival on the island, the building of the shelter, and most especially the gnoll ceremony that Shima had performed with me. He never seemed to want to look at the markings on the tree himself, so it gave me ample opportunity to come up with a celebration to surprise him. Some were straightforward: I decorated the ledge up on the cliff with flowers and shells, and convinced a puzzled Shima to eat with me up there. His simple joy at seeing the layout I had provided made my heart feel like it might burst. And some more playful: I made a trail of seashells when Shima was off doing something, and had it lead to where I shyly awaited him, a naked offering on hands and knees willing to do whatever he wished.

One I planned well ahead of time. I had a very specific thing I wanted to do, and I had no idea how long it would take. The problem was finding time to work on it without Shima knowing, and since we were together practically all the time, it was often difficult. I had located a large piece of driftwood, soft enough to carve with the knife. Surreptitiously I found opportunities to work on it, slowly moulding it into shape. Once it was complete, I was pleasantly surprised—to a true craftsman it might look crude, but to me it resembled Shima and I was proud of it. When the day came, I asked him to watch the sunset with me atop the cliff. I had hidden it up there, and as he watched curiously, seated with legs dangling off the ledge, I retrieved it from beneath the leaves where it had been hidden, and presented it to him.

It made my heart hurt—in a good way!—to see his reaction. He was absolutely thrilled, and to my surprise, he started to cry. He

reached for me, smothering me in his embrace and saying things so rapidly in gnollish that I didn't have a hope of understanding him. It made me tear up too to know how happy I had made him. He eventually released me, which was fortunate since I had been having trouble breathing, then sat back and turned over the sculpture in his hands, examining it.

"I'm glad you like it, Shima," I smiled.

"Shima loves it! Shima loves Kunet too," he replied joyfully, and I had to deal with another extensive hug as I attempted unsuccessfully to extricate myself.

His tear-streaked face met my gaze, and I kissed him.

He went back to examining his likeness happily, and then I saw his head tilt, and he slowly turned to face me, his face serious.

"Kunet make Shima's sheath too small!" he stated. His ear twitched.

"Oh? I thought it should have been smaller," I retorted with a grin.

He gasped in mock surprise.

"What did Kunet say?" he asked, slowly, dangerously.

"Well, I could have sworn it was smaller..." I started, and then I leapt up to race down the trail, a gnoll hot on my heels.

I made it to the beach before he tackled me, and I could hardly stop laughing.

"Shima will show Kunet!" he declared, and, well, the rest of the evening we were quite occupied. I eventually admitted I was wrong, of course. It was hard to resist his extremely persuasive arguments. It was a fight I was happy to lose, after all.

We had everything we needed, and honestly, everything we

wanted. I suppose it was idyllic, but it was not without its dangers. Our third year on the island was harder than most.

Shima gave us fair warning. His ears were flattened against his head, his mane was fluffed up, and he looked nervous, constantly lifting his muzzle to sniff at the air. I could sense nothing, and after this had occurred several times that morning, I asked him about it.

"What's wrong, Shima? You've looked nervous all day."

"Shima is not certain. The wind smells wrong. The sky looks wrong. The air feels wrong."

"Wrong how?"

He shrugged and continued to glance up at the sky. Now I was nervous too.

As the day progressed I understood why. The sky grew dark with clouds, and with a shudder I recalled the day the *ghaftu* came to my—no, our—villages. Shima had looked more and more unhappy, so together we retreated to our shelter, hoping to ride it out. I was glad we had set it up leeward of the cliff, but Shima's obvious consternation worried me just the same.

The wind increased rapidly, and we huddled together as the rain slashed sideways. Even all the way in the back of our shelter we still were getting wet, and I knew it would only get worse. The temperature had dropped and I shivered, even in Shima's embrace. Suddenly he looked around, panicked.

"What? What is it?" I asked.

"Where is Shima statue?"

"Shima, it doesn't matter. I can make another one, don't worry about it!" I insisted. I knew it was still up on the cliff—Shima liked to keep it there, looking out over the sea. I hadn't thought to go and grab it before the storm hit.

"No, statue is important! Shima will be back!" he exclaimed, and ran hunched over against the wind out of the shelter and out of sight.

"Shima!" I called, but the noise of the storm drowned me out. So, I waited. He did not return, so I waited longer, and my mind started to invent all the awful possibilities until I could not stand it anymore.

I went out to look for him.

Looking back on it, I know how foolish it was. The storm was almost full force, and the rain whipped at me hard enough that I was surprised it didn't draw blood. I could barely see, let alone hear anything above the roar of the storm, and I staggered towards the path that led out to the beach.

I didn't get far. There was a loud crack and I turned, but everything went black.

I have no solid recollection of what followed. There were brief moments of blurriness, but most was darkness and pain. I discovered, later, that I was unconscious for most of the next several days. When I finally regained some semblance of lucidity, my vision was all distorted. There was a Shima-esque shape that wavered before me, and it felt like I was lying upon soft earth, much like the mossy place atop the cliff. Which apparently it was, based on the unfocused forms of the nearby trees.

I must have made a noise, because the Shima-shape started making noise and nuzzling at me, and the pain was blinding. I cried out and he stopped; I was still conscious, at least, and tried to form words.

"Shima?" I managed.

"Shima is so sorry! Shima leave Kunet and tree hit Kunet and Kunet is hurt and Kunet asleep for days and Shima not know what to do and Shima look for pain herbs but not know how many herbs and Kunet is sleeping too much and Shima think Kunet is dead and Shima still not know what to do and please get better because Shima is alone and afraid and Kunet and Shima one beautiful thing but broken when not together and Shima not want to be just Shima because Shima not want to be broken."

I laid there and attempted to process this but failed.

"Shima?" I asked again, trying to focus. "I hurt, Shima…"

"Shima is sorry! Kunet is hurt because Kunet's head… injured. A tree hit Kunet. Shima is careful and tried to help. Carry Kunet up cliff, where the ground is soft with moss. Shima should get herbs for Kunet? How many herbs?"

He had to ask me this several times for me to understand, and as best I could I explained to him how to properly prepare the nightroot. I think I blacked out again for a while, but when I awoke Shima was there, and he persuaded me to swallow the paste he had in the palm of his hand. The pain faded, briefly, and in that brief window of focus before the nightroot stole it away I managed to ascertain what had occurred. Gingerly, I touched where Shima had said I was struck, and felt the fracture. It wasn't horrible, but it was on my head, and I couldn't help but wonder if there was anything I had lost. My limbs started to feel numb, a sign that the nightroot would soon pull me into sleep, so as I faded, I tried to express to Shima that I'd be okay. He had been crying the entire time I was speaking to him, and I desperately wanted to get up to hug him, but my limbs wouldn't obey me. Night fell, or things went black, I don't know.

When I next awoke, it was night. The pain was faint, and I blinked my eyes into focus. I could see the stars, and I just laid there for a time, quietly, watching them slowly travel their arc. I tilted my head, and saw Shima lying beside me, curled up. His back was to me, but he was pressed against my side—I could feel the heat of him. I reached an arm over to him, and gently caressed his side. Instantly he was awake, and his concerned face was inches from my own.

"Kunet is okay?"

"I think so, Shima. I'm sorry,"

"Why sorry? Shima is sorry, Shima is sorry Shima left Kunet alone. Shima won't do that ever again."

Speaking was exhausting, so I just kissed his nose. He shifted closer, and carefully pulled me into his embrace. He just held me quietly, and it was not long before the stars blurred again as I drifted into sleep.

The next day I felt more like myself. Shima was puppy-like in his excitement as I managed to sit up, and I had to fend him off a few times. At my request he brought me some cooked fish and water; I was famished. I managed to move far enough that I could sit with Shima on the ledge overlooking the ocean. The effort caused my head occasional sharp pulses of pain, and I seriously doubted I could make it the few paces back to the mossy earth by myself. I noticed he was very careful to have his hands on me, in case I lost my balance or fainted.

As we sat there quietly, the pain slowly faded, and out of the corner of my eye I saw Shima constantly glancing over at me. I looked over at him—his ears were back, and his expression was full of concern.

"What's wrong?" I asked.

"Kunet almost died," he responded, his voice threatening to break.

"I'm okay, Shima! It's all right." I hugged him, and he appeared somewhat mollified, though his ears still betrayed his uncertainty. "I couldn't leave you, you know that," I added. He nodded and gave me a shaky smile.

"Shima, what happens to gnolls when they die?" I asked, curiously.

"They don't move around as much," Shima responded, straight-faced. An ear twitched.

"You know what I mean! What do the gods say happens? When gnolls die?"

"Oh! All fourteen gnoll war gods also say they don't move around as much."

I glared up at him; he was grinning at me.

"Shima missed making jokes to Kunet. Kunet didn't listen to Shima's jokes much when Kunet was hurt. But Shima didn't feel like making jokes then either."

I hugged him, and he continued.

"Gnolls always been close to nature and world around village. Gnoll gods say that gnolls part of nature, like... nature spirits? Shima is not sure. That's what <kishpsibi> say. Some <kishpsibi> can see gnoll spirits, it needs special... what is word, connection? Anyway, when gnolls die, gnoll spirit joins nature, then live as nature spirit. What about humans?"

I shrugged. "It's said we get to join the sky god, Aea, when we die."

Shima was quiet for a moment.

"That sounds boring," he stated.

"What?"

"Boring. Nothing up there! Sit around in sky? What is there to do?"

"I have no idea, Shima. That's just what our shamans say."

"Shima would prefer to be spirit in nature. Nature is exciting and beautiful and wonderful. Sky has... clouds sometimes? Not very interesting."

"Well, probably not the clouds. The stars are supposed to be our ancestors, and so when we die there is a new star. That's what I mean by sky god."

He pondered that briefly.

"No, Shima still prefer nature spirit. Stars stuck there."

"The stars move!" I protested.

"No, stars all move at same time," he said. "Stars never get closer together or further apart. So, stars very lonely."

I chuckled, and indicated I agreed. "Nature spirit does sound better, you're right," I smiled.

"It is good that Kunet is gnoll now then. Short gnoll though," he grinned.

"Gnoll only in name by your ceremony!" I laughed.

Shima shrugged. "Shima still love Kunet, even if Kunet very strange-looking gnoll," he smiled.

Another two days passed before I felt well enough to take the trail back down to the beach. Evidence of the storm's passing was everywhere, with ripped up vegetation and downed trees. Most of our firepit stones had been washed away. I started down our path towards the shelter with some dread, and Shima's flattened ears and dipped tail forewarned me.

The shelter was destroyed. It had collapsed, and some of the larger logs were broken by the fall of a tree. All of the smaller pieces had been strewn about. I started to move broken vegetation at one corner of the shelter.

"Why is Kunet digging?" Shima asked.

"My writing was in here. And the knife. And our ceremony necklaces. I want to make sure they're okay," I answered, as I continued to pull away branches. My head was starting to hurt again.

"Let Shima do it," he said, gently pushing me aside. I sat back and watched as he dug through the remains of our shelter. It didn't take him long, and I was relieved to see that all of our items—including my 'barks', as Shima still described them—seemed undamaged. We moved our things to the top of the cliff, where they joined the little statue I had carved—apparently Shima had managed to rescue it. We stayed there for most of the next few weeks while I recovered enough to be useful again. It took a long time for me to heal, even as young as I was, and for years to come I would get sudden piercing headaches. Shima was very sensitive to them—he could tell almost immediately if one was starting, whether by my scent or what I do not know, but he would make me stop whatever I was doing. He would force me to rest while he sat, his amber eyes on me, a guardian against any afflictions that might dare to attack.

Hut

"A hut," Shima declared.

"What?"

"A hut. Small home? Has walls? A roof? Kunet is forgetting things again?"

I laughed. "No, I know what a hut is."

"Shima and Kunet should make a hut. Shelter is destroyed, but should not build a shelter again. Shelter was for short time, what is word… temporary. Shima and Kunet are not leaving island, island is home. So. Shima and Kunet need home on home," Shima explained.

I had to admit it sounded appealing. It had been a moon since the storm, and we had been busy clearing the area where the shelter had been with the expectation that we'd replace it. We hadn't been in any particular hurry, since too much exertion would make my head hurt.

"It'd have to be a pretty big hut," I commented. Shima cocked his head at me, puzzled. "Well, you're a pretty big gnoll," I added.

Shima grinned. "Yes, a big hut is good. But with hut it will feel like true home. Can decorate hut. Hut will have place to sleep, for both Shima and Kunet together. With soft grasses and moss and leaves. Place to play too, where Shima can remind Kunet how Shima is big gnoll. In case Kunet forgets again." He gave me a mischievous glance, and I blushed.

"That sounds perfect, Shima. It'll take a while, though," I warned.

"Is okay. Shima is not in any hurry. Shima has Kunet here, so Shima is happy."

I was right; it did take a while. It was several moons of work at our rather leisurely pace, but as it neared completion and we could see it come together, our last few days went excitedly and rapidly. It was large—easily big enough for us both. We had dug a narrow circular trench to outline where the walls would be, such that we could place the logs we had cut and shaped with one end buried, much like a palisade. It gave the walls that extra sturdiness once we bound the logs together, and we hoped it would prevent the hut from blowing over should another bad storm happen upon us. The roof was trickier but we eventually managed, and we wove multiple layers of protection with grasses and leaves to protect against the rain. We even constructed a bedframe of sorts, low to the ground, that acted as a container for the grasses and moss that we'd sleep on. We tested it that night, of course, and both agreed it would be a perfectly valid substitution for those nights where 'starwatching' was susceptible to weather.

We also added a firepit to the clearing near our hut. That first night together, enfolded within our hut, entwined with each other, with the embers of our fire a friendly glow just outside—I truly felt protected and safe.

The hut was also a safe place for the little Shima sculpture, our ceremony necklaces, my sheafs of bark, and the two stones

Shima had rescued after my failed divination. The sheafs I decided to work on the following morning, and as I sat there writing, Shima wandered off. He returned eventually with an armload of shells, presumably from some of his collection caches that dotted our island, which he poured into a pile, then grinned at me and left again. The next time he returned with his arms full of leafy branches I didn't fully recognise, so I asked him about them.

"Sticky!" he pronounced, but didn't elaborate.

He set to work on the outer walls of the hut, making grooves in seemingly random locations, and testing the placing of shells against them. Snapping some of the small branches he had brought apparently yielded a sap-like substance, which he then proceeded to use to help secure his seashells to the wood. The placement seemed haphazard, scattered randomly across the walls, but their opalescence and colours sparkled in the sunlight that filtered through the canopy above. I told him it was looking pretty and received a broad grin in return.

Time passed, and I glanced up from time to time to witness how the shells slowly spread across the hut. At one point there was some muffled gnoll cursing; apparently Shima had managed to stick several shells to his fur by mistake and was shaking his hand to attempt to get another one off. He stopped when he realised I was watching, and his glare and raised hackles told me I should definitely not be laughing. I failed at this and was forced to attempt to escape to the beach. I failed at that too, being somewhat slower than Shima, and so we ended up going for a swim for a while as I helped him extricate the shells.

A wet Shima decided he wanted to look for more shells, so I went to retrieve my bark and seated myself on a fallen tree upon

the sand, one recently felled by the storm. That way we both kept each other company in a way—since we could see each other—and from time to time I would glance up to see him gleefully picking out seashells from beneath the waves.

I still loved watching him. He would notice me doing so from time to time and happily call out, "Kunet!" Eventually he wandered further down the beach, almost around the curve of the island, so I looked down at the blank piece of bark in my hands.

It had been harder to write anything as time passed. What was I to write? In the beginning, well, there were many things that were unresolved. But now? We knew who we were, Shima and I, and we knew our home was here. We were certain of things, and were now just living our lives with each other. I could write about events, like the storm, or building our hut, but most of our time was just...us. We were simply happy and content. It is a thing I have not been able to put into words; any attempt at its representation here, with these scratches upon bark, would be a mere reflection.

On occasion, of course, I would think of my village. There was a guilt there, because I did not know what had happened and had let that part of my life go. In doing so, was I letting them down? Betraying them somehow? As I had a few times before, I decided to write some words and set them afloat upon the waves. Let them know that I was alive and I was happy, even though I had no way to get home. And hope that perhaps someday they would see those words.

I was absorbed in my writing, my gaze downward at the bark as I carved my barely legible scratches into it, when a pair of gnoll paws came into view, followed by a cold nose in my ear.

"Kunet is still writing barks? What about?"

I looked up at him, and his ear twitched. "The same kind of things. You, me, our life here. Thoughts for my village," I said warily, expecting a typically Shima response. He didn't disappoint.

"Did Kunet write about gnoll pups yet?"

"What?"

"Gnoll pups," he reiterated. His ear twitched again, so I sighed resignedly.

"What gnoll pups?"

"How Kunet wants gnoll pups. Kunet keeps asking Shima for them," he said, expression flat.

"What do you mean?" I asked.

"Oh, Shima, again!" he cried, mimicking my voice perfectly from our lovemaking the night before.

I blushed furiously, struck briefly speechless.

"Shima keeps trying! Again and again, but no gnoll pups. Shima even tries both ends!" He grinned.

"Shi—"

"Many times! Many *many* times!"

"Shima, that's not how it—"

"Shima even puts it all over Kunet when Kunet asks Shima to. That not work either! Shima thinks Kunet is broken."

I growled in mock fury and chased him across the sand, where he eventually let me tackle him, laughing at my attempts. I had to catch my breath, but entangled in his arms he smelled of sea and sand and Shima and I needed him close. So, I let him try again there on the beach, as the sun set.

Arrival

"The mind often conjures dangers where none might be found."
Tumari Proverb

The moon turned and turned again. I did not count them, just simply marked them upon the tree. Shima, as always, seemed pointedly uninterested in the passage of time.

Our hut proved both sturdy and cozy. The feel of an enclosed, safe place, along with the friendly glow of our fire just outside, made it a welcome alternative to the moss atop the cliff. Most of our nights were spent at the latter, for the open sky above and, well, it was *our* place. But for times when things were... gentler, quieter, closer? The hut served us well.

Its sturdiness was proven with its steadfastness through another storm. It was not quite as severe as the one where I was injured, but it was still a matter of concern. Shima sensed its approach, once again, and was insistent I stay inside and safe before it even arrived. He even stood guard in the entryway of our hut, as if he could somehow prevent the storm from coming in or attacking me. My initial amusement at this was soon replaced with deep affection for him; he was so concerned about my safety his ears were plastered to his head for the entirety of the night, and he would not sleep, but watch me to make certain I was all right.

There was some minor damage; some of Shima's shells had become unglued, while some of the roof thatch and leaves had been torn away in the winds. But those were both easily fixed with little difficulty the following day. Aea was prone to fits of anger, yes, but once he had raged it was as if nothing had happened. The skies were clear and blue, and Shima ended up spending the next few days searching the shallows for new shells that might have arrived, for Aea's anger often coincided with Û's fury, churning the sea with new detritus and treasures to find.

I helped of course, but it was more to keep him company. I would occasionally leave him to his shells and use some of the time either clearing some of the storm debris from our clearing and path or searching for different things for dinner. Fish every evening could be repetitive, so both of us loved to mix things up as much as we could within the rather limited set of possibilities.

So I went looking for berries.

Shima was busy spearward down the beach, but most of the berry bushes I had found in the past were inland and starward, so I headed that way. Many had been blown almost bare of fruit in the recent storm, but I did find some closer to the beach after wandering through the jungle. I found plenty, more than sufficient for a meal or two, and was about to head back to see what Shima was up to when I noticed something out at sea.

Something about it sent a frisson down my spine, and I crouched there, hidden behind the bushes at the edge of the sands, trying to discern what it was.

A boat. And figures upon it.

And it was coming closer, that was evident. It had a sail, possibly crab-claw, but was clearly damaged. A catamaran, it seemed, but larger than the one I had been entrusted years ago. And the figures? I could make them out now. Three of them—gnolls.

I don't remember my panicked run back towards our stretch of beach. I stood there on the sand, near our firepit, only then becoming aware of the cuts and scratches I had suffered in my sprint through the rainforest. Shima had noticed me—he was in sight, near where the island started to curve—and his head was cocked curiously as he approached.

It was then that I found I had absolutely no idea what to say. I was suddenly filled with apprehension—these were gnolls. What would Shima think? What would he do? Would he be happy to see them? Would he be so ecstatic to be amongst his own kind that I would be set aside and forgotten? I felt a bit dizzy, and it got worse as I began to panic again, the possibilities swarming inside me until I could not think coherently. All I could focus upon was the selfish hope that the gnolls might depart before Shima would see them.

Shima hurried the last several steps upon seeing my obvious discomfort, and embraced me.

"Kunet? Is Kunet okay?"

"Shima…" I managed.

"Is Kunet's head? Hurt again?"

My headaches from the injury were thankfully few and far between now, but it was still a concern when they occurred, for both of us. I shook my head.

"No, Shima, I'm okay. Sorry. Just a bit dizzy."

He looked at me, his amber eyes filled with worry, and sat me down on the sand.

"Kunet should sit." He sat next to me, and glanced at me often to make sure I was okay, while I was quiet, unable to avoid contemplating all the horrible things that might occur due to the presence of these new gnolls. Shima knew something was bothering me, but didn't know how to ask, and I didn't know how to tell him.

So we sat in silence, and the sun slowly crept lower.

The wind shifted slightly, and Shima immediately became alert, raising himself to a crouch.

"Shima smells... gnolls?" He sounded confused and excited and wary, all at once. He looked down at me.

My lack of response was telling, and I could feel him staring at me. Out of the corner of my eye, I saw him stand, and I glanced up. He was just looking at me, his face expressionless. But to me he looked hurt—hurt that I hadn't told him. Saying nothing, he started off down the beach towards the boulders where he kept his pigments. It was too far away for me to observe what he was doing, and once I had collected myself, I made my way over to where he was. I wanted to explain.

He was mixing his paints, and it was not long before he had started decorating himself. The designs were sharp and angular, almost tooth-like, and they directed attention towards his face. He met my eyes, all purple and yellow lines—he looked ferocious.

"Why Kunet not tell Shima?"

"I..." I wasn't sure how to explain myself. And my delay seemed to answer him.

"Kunet should stay here," he stated flatly, and set off starwards along the beach, pausing only to pick up his spear from where it lay beside the firepit.

I sat there by our firepit a long time.

My mind was a turmoil, as if Û's anger churned within, bouncing my thoughts this way and that with the waves like they were so much flotsam. I could not hold onto a thought, but only worry about what might happen. Was happening, I reminded myself. Was Shima all right? Would he find that camaraderie amongst his fellow gnolls that I could not provide?

As the sun set, I fished. The berries I had collected lay forgotten near the firepit—I had no desire to eat them without Shima there. I made sure to find enough fish for us both, but as night fell, I ended up eating my portion alone.

The stars made themselves known, and I watched them turn. The unmoving star, the starward one, the one that stood alone as the others turned around it, sat above the beach in the direction Shima had gone. I sighed and made my way up the cliff. It was to sleep, I told myself, but I knew I hoped that from near that vantage I might see the gnolls. But I could not, and it took me a long time to fall asleep.

At some point during the night, Shima returned. I felt his oh-so-familiar heat and solidity press against me, and I tensed, uncertain. I shifted slightly, pretending I was asleep, and he grew still. How did my breathing sound when I was asleep? I wasn't sure, but I made my best guess. But who was I fooling? Shima would know—his senses were far sharper than mine. But I kept up the pretence anyhow, until eventually I heard Shima's soft snores.

When I awoke, dawn was barely lightening the sky. Shima was standing, putting on his loincloth, and his ears swivelled when he heard me shift.

"Hello, Kunet! Shima go to help other gnolls."

I didn't know how to feel about that, so I was quiet. Shima eyed me for a bit, then sighed.

"Kunet. Is right to help gnolls. Kunet helped Shima when Shima hurt and hungry and thirsty, yes?"

"Of course—" I began.

"Then should help new gnolls too. New gnolls hungry and thirsty. Not really hurt, but still need help."

I had no argument to that. Shima embraced me and left, while I laid upon the moss painfully conscious of all my anxieties. The dreams that had threatened me during the night still hovered there, intangible, fragments and shards swiftly dissolving, leaving behind only the unfocused emotions.

I descended to the beach, and the firepit was cold. I had no desire to fish, so I ate some of the berries and decided to set off up the beach. I wanted to see, for I was sick at heart and did not want to be alone. I had not gone far when I decided that it would be best to approach from the jungle, that way I wouldn't be seen. Why was I hiding? I wasn't sure.

By the time I had made my way close enough to catch glimpses, the sun had entered Aea's domain. There was a catamaran, pulled up onto the sands. Its crab-claw sail had been shredded, its woven reeds and leaves mostly broken or missing. It was a large boat, and was of a size the three gnolls I had seen could have easily fit upon it. I only saw two, though; both were working on the boat, attempting to thread new reeds. Shima was in the shallows, spearfishing, and a small fire was lit nearby. He stopped soon after I arrived and I watched, hidden in the foliage, as he walked up onto the sands. There was some queried conversation between him and the other gnolls—he seemed confused—but it did not seem antagonistic. I

saw no other weapons other than Shima's, which made me breathe a sigh of relief.

A relief that was interrupted by the appearance of the third gnoll, mere strides to my left. Its hackles were raised, teeth bared, and it hurtled towards me. I did not freeze, at least—my familiarity with Shima prepared me for the image of an angry gnoll, or, in Shima's case, a mock-angry gnoll. Even so, I was terrified, for I knew how physically powerful gnolls could be, and I bolted for the beach. I knew Shima was nearby and I yelled his name, fear colouring my voice.

The gnoll was barrelling through the underbrush right on my heels. I knew Shima was faster than me, so I did not doubt this particular gnoll was too; the beach seemed dreadfully far away.

I tripped and fell at about the same time that Shima appeared, his hackles as raised as I'd ever seen them. There was a snarl and grunt as Shima lunged to intercept where I had been but moments before. On hands and feet I scrabbled backwards; Shima had his hand around the throat of the other gnoll, pressing it against the trunk of a tree. It had happened blindingly fast, and I just stared. They did too—at each other—and the gnoll dipped its muzzle. Shima pushed the gnoll to one side and it stumbled, then he reached a hand down to help me to my feet.

The other gnoll headed back towards the beach, and uncertainly, I followed Shima. We stood there, myself a step behind him and to the side, and the three gnolls stood by the catamaran, several strides away. Shima was angry—I could sense it. And hear it, from the barrage of gnollish that followed.

"<Shima *zenu'ka!* Gnolls *arni'ka-u* because *kahpru'anu Shima'i*>!" he shouted, looking at each of the gnolls in turn. I could only catch a few of the words—my gnollish was still nowhere near adept. "<Gnolls *semi-rra* and *izuzi-rra'ahnnu* because *kahpru'anu Shima'i*>!"

I stood silently, oblivious to what was being said. The gnolls stood silently too, and one by one their muzzles lowered. Now that I had a chance to observe them, I realised they seemed underfed compared to Shima—perhaps their experience at sea had been even worse than ours, I surmised. The sail certainly indicated something had happened.

In the quiet that followed, Shima turned to me. The other gnolls' ears swivelled as he spoke in my tongue. "Is okay now, Kunet. Gnolls not realise Kunet part of Shima's tribe. Gnolls see human, not know Kunet is Kunet. Gnolls weak from ocean and scared, see human spying, not know is Kunet. Shima told of Kunet before, but did not think to say no other humans."

"<*Awil'anu* Kunet>!" he continued, directing his speech towards the gnolls once again. "<Shima *Kunet'ri...hiahru'rro*>," he stated, more quietly but firmly, and their heads tilted quizzically. They all turned to look at me, then back at him.

"That one, that is Fhhru. Fhhru chase Kunet," he said to me, gifting the gnoll a brief glare. "That one, that is Hrrii, Hrrii female. Others male. Last one, that is Seka. All from gnoll village, different village somewhere, not Shima's village. Storm hit village hard, three gnolls lost, many days. Shima helping gnolls get food, get water, but gnolls know this Shima's island. Kunet's too," he added, giving me a smile.

"What did you tell them just now?" I asked, and my voice sounded small compared to the richness that was Shima's gnollish. It made me feel even more self-conscious.

"That gnolls should obey, this Shima's place. And that Kunet is Kunet, and that Kunet is Shima's mate and part of Shima's village."

I could feel the heat rise to my face at that, in a mixture of embarrassment and appreciation that Shima had named me as such, and I nodded, unsure if my voice would work right then. He was silent for a moment, and as the seconds passed, I felt more and more awkward with the eyes of all the gnolls upon me. Shima, as always, sensed my discomfiture.

"New gnolls can make fire. Shima found fish for gnolls. Kunet and Shima go fish? Make fire, have food?"

I nodded to that, and after a quick spurt of gnollish between Shima and the others, he and I made our way back to our stretch of the beach. He set immediately to the fire and I hunted the shallows in search of prey. The fire was burning merrily by the time I approached, fish in hand, and Shima was eyeing me critically.

"Kunet hurt? Fhhru hurt Kunet?"

All the scratches on my body were from my panicked rush through the rainforest the previous day, and I told him so. He was quiet, watching me, and I knew he could scent my uncertainty. I didn't know what to make of the other gnolls, especially after the thwarted attack, and Shima was quite clever at discerning things.

"Is okay, Kunet. Fhhru understand now, Kunet safe. Gnolls not want fight, gnolls just scared. Gnolls know this Shima's and Kunet's place. Gnolls want to leave, go back to gnoll home."

I was quiet, but nodded.

"And Shima help gnolls with water and food. And boat. So gnolls leave soon," he added.

"All right," I said, but I was still unsure. I could not tell if he wanted to leave too, and he hadn't told me one way or the other.

We ate our meal in companionable, though stressed, silence, even as Shima tried to get me to smile, nudging me repeatedly, but unable to fully hide the tilt of his ears that heralded his concern.

"Kunet come help too?"

The sun was near its apex when we made our way back along the beach towards our visitors. It had taken some time for me to pluck up the courage to accompany Shima, but he was patient and content to wait, taking the time to wash off the paint from the previous day, explaining it was no longer needed.

All three were there, near the boat, and there was a flurry of gnollish back and forth that barely impinged on my thoughts, confused as they were. Eventually I realised Shima was talking to me.

"Kunet okay?"

"Sorry, Shima, I was thinking of something else."

"Kunet know boat, yes? Shima remembers Kunet describing Kunet boat from long ago."

I nodded.

"Kunet help Hrrii? Gnolls not know fixing sail, Kunet help?"

I didn't protest, so after some further gnollish conversation, Shima took the other two gnolls with him to search for necessary reeds and leaves as sail material. I was left with Hrrii. She smiled with too many teeth.

First we needed to recover what we could from the existing sail. Much of it was broken and ripped—most of the leaves were torn and useless. Some of the woven reeds were salvageable, and I helped direct Hrrii to which ones we could reuse.

"<No, that one there>," I mentioned at one point, in my very basic gnollish.

Her ears went straight up as she whipped her head around to stare at me. I struggled to remember what I knew.

"<Sorry>?" I managed.

She laughed. She seemed thrilled, her ears going every which way, and her tongue lolled. A stream of gnollish followed and I blinked, not understanding a word of it.

"<Kunet speak very little gnoll. Kunet speak badly,>" I said, carefully, stumbling through it slowly. She grinned.

"<Kunet *awil'panu* Hrrii hear speak! Is good!>" she stated, clearly trying to use the simplest words she could.

Well, after that, she kept pushing at me. I didn't mind—her enthusiasm was infectious, and reminded me a little bit of Shima. Soon, we were doing our best to keep up a conversation as we worked, and when the rest returned, I was a source of much interest and amusement from the other two at my basic attempts at their language. Shima just grinned, refusing to help, and I glared at him.

The afternoon passed quicker than I expected, and I was convinced my gnollish was better near the end of it. When Shima suggested we join them for a meal as the sun set, I had no qualms about doing so. It was interesting watching them as we all sat around the fire. Tone, inflection, body language, physical differences—after knowing Shima for so long, it was quite easy for me to see them as individual gnolls with their own characteristics and quirks. Yet as the evening continued, even though I would be encouraged to join the conversation—mainly by Shima and Hrrii—I could not help but feel like more and more an outsider. Listening to the musicality and depth of tone in their language as they spoke amongst each other...well, I felt as if it was something

I couldn't truly attain. My voice was not made for those sounds, and as I watched Shima's joy at truly using his language again, I hurt for him that he had been without it so long.

I think it was his name that affected me most.

As always, like when he spoke to me, Shima would use his name when referring to himself. He did the same when speaking to the other gnolls. Yet the difference was how he pronounced it—it was that original, impossible-for-me-to-voice name that he introduced himself as, so long ago. It made it seem that the 'Shima' he used for me was a mere reflection, a crude copy of the true name he had, and there was something about that that made me suddenly feel unutterably sad.

I knew all the gnolls would pick up on my emotions sooner rather than later, so I excused myself, apologised in gnollish, and headed back to our hut. Shima's eyes glittered in the night as I departed, reflecting the dancing flames.

I dreamt.

We had repaired the gnolls' catamaran, and set sail. The sky was too blue, the day too perfect. There was a true camaraderie between all of us, and I did not feel excluded at all. I even seemed to understand most of the gnollish, and all encouraged me to speak more.

Our sail rippled with Aea's blessing and the sea glittered as we headed dawnwards. We paused to fish, for the gnolls were getting hungry, and here in the deep ocean they found fish of colours and shapes that I had never seen before. I helped too, attempting to fish alongside them, but all I could find were oysters. Even when I would catch a fish, as soon as I brought it to the edge of the boat it was another oyster, and I was growing frustrated. Soon there was a pile of them, and Shima laughed along with the others.

We hoisted the sail once more, and the ocean passed us by quicker than was possible. I busied myself prying open oysters, only to find nothing inside. Each was an empty shell. Until one: it contained Shima's necklace. I realised then that he had not been wearing it, and I was not wearing the other half. I handed it to him.

"Shima's necklace!" he said, and nosebumped me. He put it on. "Where Kunet's necklace?"

I didn't know. "I'm... trying to find it, Shima."

I could see the distant shore approaching much too fast. How could we have reached it so soon? Frantically, I prised apart more oysters even as the pile seemed to grow bigger, and each was empty. I looked up; Shima was chatting amiably with the others, and I felt more and more isolated as each oyster's shell yielded up nothing.

"Kunet? Where is Kunet's necklace?" Shima looked hurt, and I couldn't speak, even as I tried. Panicked, I kept digging through the oysters as Shima returned to his gnoll companions on the other catamaran. *Other?* I thought, and suddenly noticed I was aboard my old catamaran from back at the village, sailing parallel to the gnolls' larger one.

"<There's our village>!" called Hrrii, and slowly their craft curved away towards it. Mine refused to turn, and gradually our paths diverged.

"Kunet? Why isn't Kunet wearing necklace?" asked Shima, as he stood atop the other catamaran, just out of my reach.

"Shima! Wait, please, I'll find it!" I begged, as my tears began to fall.

He looked at me, his face full of sadness and disappointment, and turned away.

"Shima!" I cried, and their catamaran slowly grew smaller with the distance, my other half upon it.

I awoke then and could feel Shima pressed against me. Relief swept through me, and I started to cry, clutching him to me. Wordlessly he held me, and I must have fallen asleep quickly, because I remember little else.

The morning found me mostly smothered by Shima—he was half-sprawled on top of me, snoring, when I awoke. Wriggling out was impossible without waking him, and he sleepily pulled me closer when I made the attempt. I resigned myself to being pressed against him, which of course I didn't mind. I laid there, failing to rid myself of the dream's touch, and worried. When he awoke, I tried to convince him everything was fine, though he seemed skeptical.

He pretended not to notice my mood as we ate our morning meal, spending most of it discussing his intent to further work on repairs with the others. I knew he was trying to distract me from my worries, so I set my mind to being happy for him and his opportunity for company, and followed him starward along the beach.

All three hailed us as we approached, and soon we had slipped into our roles from the day previous. Hrrii happily chattered away, and I attempted to keep up, which thankfully helped me to focus on something other than my concerns. It was mid-afternoon by the time we pronounced the catamaran fit to ride the ocean once more. Through Shima I learned that the gnolls wanted to collect food for all of us, and bid us return when the sun set.

I headed for our hut, unsure what to do, and sat there, mind adrift, while Shima hummed to himself outside, poking at the nearby firepit. Eventually, his head appeared by the hut's opening.

"Okay, Kunet. What is wrong?" He crouched in the entryway, arms folded.

I let it all flood forth. How it was wonderful to see his happiness at being amongst his fellows. How there were aspects of being a gnoll I could never understand or share with him. How I could never pronounce his name as it should be. At that, I started to cry, and I expressed my worry that I didn't know if he wanted to leave our island so he could be amongst gnolls again, and what would that mean for me, and would he want me to come too.

He made his way inside and held me for a long moment.

"Shima has an idea," he said, after a while. "Perhaps ask gods what Shima should do?"

I gave him a puzzled look.

"Follow Shima!" he stated, and made his way out of the hut and towards the beach. I followed in his wake, and he bade me sit across from him in the wet sand by the sea.

"Shima, you made fun of my divination attempt last time," I said unhappily.

He scowled at that. "Shima not make fun. Shima never joke," he stated firmly. "Anyway, Shima have rocks!" He opened his palm, displaying the two rocks he must have grabbed from our hut as we left: the bright green one and the small dark one. "Ready?"

"Shima, we need more rocks than that…"

"Why? Gods didn't answer last time. Maybe gods confused because too many rocks."

"That's not how it works though."

"Oh? Kunet know what gods think?"

"Of course not, Shima."

"Well. Shima thinks Kunet's gods strange because they like rocks so much. But Shima's turn to do divination, so Shima will do it Shima's way."

I chuckled. "All right, go ahead."

He stared at me, amber eyes on my own, intently serious. He tossed the stones.

"Hmm. Hmmm." He cocked his head, as if to look at it from another angle. "Hmmmm."

I laughed. "Shima, stop fooling around."

"Shima not fooling! Anyway, divination is clear. See?" He pointed at the two stones sitting there on the sand.

I looked down at them then up at him, expectantly.

"Green stone and dark stone together! That mean Shima and Kunet should be together."

"But there are only two—" I started, but he interrupted.

"Will do again! Make sure." He snatched up the stones and waited for the surf to wipe the sand clean. He threw them down.

"Oh, look!" His exaggerated expression of surprise pulled another chuckle from me. "Shima-stone and Kunet-stone are next to each other again! What could it mean?" He stared at my face, waiting. Just as I was about to answer, he interrupted, "Shima knows! It means Shima and Kunet should be together. And *will* be together," he said softly, intently, meeting my eyes. I couldn't look away.

"And look, Kunet's other question? Leave island? Answered also with stones," he said, looking back down at them. "Stones together, but where are stones? Sitting on beach on island!"

"Well of course they are!" I laughed. "You put them there!"

"So, that mean Shima and Kunet stay on island. Together. As it should be." He looked up at me again, and the depth of affection in those amber eyes made me start to cry.

"Oh, Shima…" I managed, and he held me close for a long time.

I carried with me a much lighter heart as we headed to meet our visitors. They had managed to obtain quite the feast: not many fish since none had spears, but crab and mussels and oysters in very sizeable quantities. Even enough for four hungry gnolls, I thought.

The fire was bright, the stars were bright, and voices were bright. I was content to sit quietly, wedged between Shima and Seka, and just listen to them all talk amongst themselves. I could pick out a word or two, but rarely enough to follow any thread in the continuous sing-song of conversation. Still, it did not matter. Shima was happy, and I was happy for him to have this time amongst them.

At one point, the tone changed. A query from Fhhru, voice serious but soft, and the gnolls, including Shima, were silent for a moment. Fhhru continued, and I heard my name mentioned—he was looking at me. At my obvious confusion, Shima clarified.

"Gnolls want to know if gnolls stay few more days. Boat done, but gnolls still weak and want to be strong before sailing. But gnolls know this Shima's island and Kunet's island, and so ask Shima and Kunet for permission."

It was a strange sensation—but a good one!—knowing they were asking me as well, not just Shima. All four gnolls were looking at me, their eyes reflecting the firelight. I nodded.

"<Fhhru and Hrrii and Seka stay and be strong>," I managed, doing my best with my limited vocabulary. Happily, the relieved expressions meant I was understood, and I couldn't help but notice that four gnolls grinning is a *lot* of teeth.

"Fhhru also wants Kunet to know Fhhru sorry Fhhru attack. Fhhru say Fhhru not know Kunet was Kunet," Shima informed me.

"<Things okay. Gnolls friends now>," I said, and Fhhru seemed pleased.

As talk dwindled down to quiet companionship, Shima and I bade our fellows goodnight and walked unhurriedly back down the beach. I was quiet and Shima was humming to himself, when he suddenly exclaimed, "Kunet!"

"What?"

"Shima thinks there is another divination." He pulled me along, heading over to where we had left the stones earlier. I was glad they were still there; I hadn't thought to put them back in the hut, and they could have been lost with the tide.

"Hmmmm," pondered Shima as we got close. I looked at him, then over at the stones. He must have repositioned them before we left earlier, without me noticing.

The green stone was on top of the dark one.

"Shima knows what that means!" He grabbed the stones in one hand and my hand in the other.

I laughed, and let myself be dragged up the cliff path. I lay on the moss, and Shima was above me, his shape silhouetted against the stars above. Eagerly he mounted me, and I held him close when his heat gushed forth. He was by no means done, and I did not care if the noises I could not help but make were heard on the beach starward, far below.

Changes

"The flame burns just as bright, just as hot, until all the wood is gone."
Gnoll Proverb

The next few days were lazy ones.

Shima and I would wander over to the gnolls' stretch of the beach in the morning and help them fish. Fhhru expressed interest in the spearfishing process, so Shima lent him his spear; I ended up spending quite a bit of time showing him the tricks I'd learned, and he eagerly followed my direction.

Midday I would leave Shima and the gnolls to converse—I knew it was something he desperately wanted, though he never said as such. I felt if I were there he would worry about me and spend his time making certain I was involved, so I'd make my way back to our hut. After Shima's 'divinations', I was no longer concerned that he'd want to leave, but I hoped his time with his fellows would ease some of the ache of being apart from his kind.

Shima would come find me during the afternoon, and we'd help the gnolls with additional items that might come in useful upon the ocean. Hrrii and Fhhru joined Shima in felling a tree and shaping an oar, while I spent time alone with Seka, collecting reeds and leaves should their sail become damaged at sea. We'd also collect larger leaves and vines for wrapping food that they could take along, for finding food out in the deep ocean would be difficult.

Seka struck me as a quiet sort, and I think the language barrier made it worse. He spoke up, though, on our second afternoon of foraging.

"<Kunet>?"

I looked over at him. He was standing there, and he had the body language that I'd seen before in Shima when he was uncertain how to say something. His muzzle was dipped slightly and he would not look straight at me.

"<Yes, Seka>?"

His ears flicked at my gnollish. "<Seka knows Shima good gnoll>," he said, purposefully attempting to simplify his speech for my benefit. I must have looked somewhat puzzled, for he continued. "<Seka sees Shima *hram'madi* Kunet. Watch Kunet>."

"<What Seka mean>?" I asked.

He paused, and it was clear he was trying to dissect whatever he wanted to tell me into the simplest words he could.

"<Seka sees Shima and Kunet. When Kunet *epesi* or busy and Kunet not see Shima, Shima sometimes watch Kunet. Seka sees Shima watch, and Shima's *qhibit'zhai* and eyes show love very much>." He was silent a moment, embarrassed. "<Seka tell Kunet so Kunet know. Good thing Kunet know. Shima good mate and happy>."

Seka stopped then, and he turned away slightly when he noticed me start to tear up.

"<Seka, Kunet thanks Seka. Kunet loves Shima very much>," I managed, my voice wavering. He nodded, satisfied, and crouched down to pick some more leaves.

Evenings found us all gathered amidst the merriment of the fire and gnollish conversation. I could not follow it, but revelled in Shima's happiness. It was Shima's time, and I wanted that for him. If the loneliness of my own thoughts, or the wondering after my own kind, or any other aches of the heart crept within, I did my best to push them aside. And when it threatened to spill over, I took my leave and left the gnolls by the fire, retreating spearward to our place atop the cliff to await Shima's return.

Fhhru, Hrrii, and Seka had arrived during the time of the moon's crescent, and the halfmoon was beginning to swell when they departed.

Shima and I were welcomed at their fire with the dawn, and we all busied ourselves collecting the remaining supplies they would need on their journey. The two of us had more bowls made of coconut shells than we needed, and though they made awkward containers on a bobbing catamaran, we all knew every little bit of water would help. Each of the three gnolls had a waterskin, and I made trips back and forth to the rill by our hut with as many bowls and waterskins as I could carry. Shima, in the meantime, was busy spearfishing with Fhhru, while Hrrii and Seka hunted down a rather large haul of crustaceans. By midmorning we all felt they were suitably supplied with food and water for a significant time at sea.

Fortunately, they also knew which way to go. Just dusk of starward was their village, Hrrii said, but she figured it would take at least several days to get there. And that was if the gods blessed them. I earnestly hoped Û would look kindly upon them all.

I fetched one final item for them to take across the ocean, which I had written during my time apart from Shima and the other gnolls.

Fhhru tried to decipher the sheaf of bark—upside-down—while I explained in my broken gnollish that it was a message for my village. My embarrassment at the request and my frustration at my communication difficulties caused Shima to step in and explain things more fully on my behalf. He spent some time telling of his own village and nearby landmarks, in the hopes that they or someone in their village would know of it—and if they could find Shima's village, they would find mine. Or its remains.

Hrrii was intense in her promise to find them. I knew all three of the gnolls were thankful for our help, but I teared up when she focused her attention on me and explained, as simply as she could, that she would do her best to get the message to my tribe. I knew I might never find out if she succeeded, but it lifted my spirits to know that there was a chance that those I cared for back home would know I was still alive. Yet it hurt as well, and my throat felt tight, because I knew then that it would be all they'd ever know of me. All Kana would ever know of me.

That left only the goodbyes.

Each of the gnolls embraced Shima in farewell, and the three of them did the same with me. We watched as they set off, the ocean excited but calm, and the stiff breeze caught their raised sail with a snap. We stood there a long time, and we could see them wave before the distance stretched too far. Shima had his arm around me, and I'm sure he was recalling, as I was, the last time we stood together and watched our raft slowly disappear into the horizon.

The mix of emotions swirling inside me attracted Shima's attention, so he kissed me and held me close. Later as the sun set and the welcome stars arose, the two of us, alone once more on the island that was to always be our home, slowly, as if we had all the time in the world, made love long into the night.

We were happy.

The sun trod the sky, the stars danced in their arcs, and the moon turned.

Those turnings became years once more, and the tree with my markings of the moon's passing was scored with tens upon tens of cuts, yet it felt like both our island and ourselves stayed much the same. Shima and I simply lived our lives together, content—and it was if we stood by each other's side and the world and sky spun around us.

Oh, there were small changes, of course, that were a natural product of time passing.

Shima couldn't stop playing with his hut decorations, either replacing or adding to what he had embedded in its walls with a new variety of shells and stones. Invariably he'd manage to either get some stuck to himself or intentionally glue some on me when I wasn't looking, but that was Shima.

There were other improvements too. Shima took it upon himself to do some more clearing with the axe, giving us more paths through the rainforest and quicker access to the further beaches, while I carved some shelves upon which our most treasured things were placed. I told Shima he was too big for me to put on the shelf, and I'd just have to have him with me all the time instead.

But, once the gnolls had left and we were alone once more, my first objective was to better speak his tongue. When I saw the joy it brought my companion when he had the other gnolls to speak with in his language, it was such an obvious thing for me to do.

"<Shima, teach Kunet>," I said, as we walked the beach a few days after the gnolls' departure.

"<Teach Kunet what>?" Shima responded, as he crouched in the shallows to grab a shell he had seen. Distracted as he was, it took a moment before he realised I had asked in gnollish. He turned and gave me a broad, toothy grin.

"<Teach Kunet more gnollish>," I said, before switching back. "I know you've taught me bits of it for fun, and I know I'm horrible at pronouncing things, but... Shima, I saw how happy you were in your own language. I want to be able to give you that."

He hugged me tight.

So, I learned. I pushed myself, because Shima would quickly sense my frustrations and wouldn't insist, so I had to demand that he stick to gnollish. It was exhausting at times, both mentally and physically—I had to work to make even shallow imitations of some of the sounds—but the pleasure at watching Shima's face and ears react to when I got something close to correct made it all worth it.

After several turnings of the moon, we even had times where I managed to stick to gnollish for the entirety of the day. Not without odd expressions and ear movements from Shima that indicated my pronunciations left something to be desired, but he was a patient teacher. He was utterly amused by the whole situation, but I could tell he very much appreciated it.

As the years slowly trickled by, it became almost as natural for me to speak in his tongue as my own, if one could ignore the fact that I just did not possess the capability for some of the sounds. It just became another facet of our life together.

There were anxious moments, of course. Years cannot pass without events, after all.

We had storms on occasion. But never with the impact of the one in which our shelter was destroyed and I was hurt. I think both Aea and Û were satisfied with what I had been through already? Perhaps they looked upon Shima and myself with kindness now, seeing our happiness. I knew they were not petty gods—the odd storm was more a reminder to acknowledge them and their power, and to not forget.

I occasionally had headaches, but they had become more and more infrequent. Even so, their onset would result in Shima suddenly appearing next to me covered in worry. Amusingly, it was easier to deal with the pain than it was to deal with an overprotective and concerned Shima. I didn't mind, though.

I got ill once or twice, and that upset Shima more than most things. He would feel helpless, and when I felt sick it was difficult for me to console him. He knew there were paintings his tribe did for sicknesses and it frustrated him to no end that he did not remember them. He came up with his own, though. Sometimes they were on himself, but a lot of the time he'd insist on using his paints on me, fretting all the time.

He never lost his sense of humour even when I was ill, but my recovery made it come out in force.

"<Shima, Kunet feels much better. No longer hot>," I said, one morning after a fever that had finally broken. He stood there, yellow bodypaint on his fur in whorls and lines—he had painted similar on myself, hoping that it might help—and was gleeful that it might have helped in my recovery.

"<So Kunet feels like proper Kunet again? Ready to walk with Shima and do all the things we do>?"

"I think so," I smiled.

"<Shima will be right back then! Don't go anywhere>."

I hadn't planned on it, so I remained lying on the grasses within our hut, awaiting his return. It took rather longer than expected, but I was still recovering my strength, so I didn't mind.

"<Okay>!" he called from outside the hut, and made his way in.

He had washed off the whorls and stood there, naked and damp. He had replaced the yellow paint with white arrows. All of which pointed to his groin. Even still weak, I couldn't help but laugh. Fortunately he was willing to wait a while before I took him up on the offer.

My tree with its markings had grown thicker and I notched another line in the wood when dawn came, for the moon had blazed in the sky in all its glory the night previous. It had shone in Shima's fur and eyes, and made the blackness of his spear glisten like obsidian where I pleasured him, as we laid beside each other on the moss atop the cliff.

I had left the scores but not counted them for a long time, so out of curiosity I did.

Twenty years. Twenty years of myself and Shima. And we had not needed, nor wanted, anything more.

I was perhaps technically past the prime of my adulthood, but I still felt as fit as ever. Shima, of course, was still the picture of hale heartiness; not once had he fallen ill, and he was just as vigorous and active as when we first started our lives together. I did notice that the spots in his tawny fur, once a rich, dark mahogany, had faded slightly over time. And of course, the greying of his muzzle.

It was only a recent development, but it was enough of a change that I pointed it out. Shima was helping me shave as he usually did, and we were seated in the wet sand across from each other, enjoying the tentative touches of the waves.

He caught me staring at him while he was carefully running the knife across my cheek, and he paused, meeting my eyes.

"<What>?"

"I see you have some white fur on your muzzle now," I remarked with a smile.

There was a brief flash of something undecipherable behind those dark amber eyes of his, and then it passed. "Yes, Shima has some white fur. Kunet should not comment unless Kunet wants his nipples mistakenly shaved off."

I laughed. "Why? I think it's cute."

Shima stopped, his expression unreadable. "Does Kunet want Shima to make a mistake while shaving Kunet's other fur?" he said, looking pointedly between my legs.

"Okay, okay! I'll stop," I chuckled, and in the days and moons to come, I avoided mentioning it, even as more of his muzzle turned grey.

He was, as always, very affectionate. But in the moons that followed, he was even more so, and there was very little time when I was alone. He would spend as much time with me as possible, even forgoing his normal seashell hunting and other such excursions in order to keep me company in whatever I might be doing. And our nights? He would exhaust me.

We had been together so long we knew exactly what each other wanted, when we spent our time beneath the stars. Often I would pleasure him, for I loved his taste, that salty earthiness that was Shima, and I savoured him as he spilled. I would then shift, laying down with my back upon the soft moss, and he would mount, my thighs against his belly as he thrust into me. Twice or more, and if I had not been brought to my own release by it, he would slide out, slick and wet, and take me into his muzzle until I cried out.

But those nights, with the new turnings of the moon? His vigour seemed unending, and when I could take no more, he would ask me to mount him too. And in the mornings when I awoke, aching from his attentions the night before, his amber eyes would be inches from my own. He would just hold me there, upon the moss, until nature's call bid us both to finally rise.

I know why now, I suppose, when I look back upon it.

We were walking along the beach one morning, and Shima expressed a desire to stop a moment. I was used to it; many times, he would suddenly see something sparkle beneath the waves, or a glint in the sand, and rush over to see what it might be while I waited. But not this time. He merely sat upon a large rock in the shallows.

"<Shima>?" I went over to him. His ears were pulled back slightly.

He grinned at me as I approached, but I had known him for too long at this point to be fooled. There was something there, in his face, in his body language. "<What is wrong>?" I asked.

"<Shima is okay>," he said, and got up to continue our walk. I stopped him, my hand on his chest, and he slowly sat back down. I sat beside him on the rock, quietly waiting. The silence stretched; I knew he knew I was waiting for him to say something—I could tell by his ears, his muzzle, the way he held himself, all the aspects of the gnoll I had been intimately close to for so long. And with the silence, as it grew longer, I began to dread. I swallowed, feeling panic start to well up from deep within me.

"Shima…?" I said, and my voice shook.

He looked over at me and sighed. "Shima is sorry, Kunet. Shima is getting tired," he admitted, and his eyes were wet.

"What do you mean, tired?" I asked, fearing what he meant but not wanting to acknowledge it. I hoped time would somehow stop so I wouldn't have to hear him answer.

"Gnolls are different than humans. Humans… live a long time. Gnolls, well, gnolls do not live as long."

I waited until I felt I could speak, but my voice still cracked. "How long?"

"Not long now," he admitted. "Gnolls are strong and fit and healthy all the way. They only weaken at the very end."

"How long have you known?"

He looked away at that, his muzzle down. "Shima has known for a little while. Shima is sorry, Kunet. So very sorry."

"Why didn't you tell me?" My tears were flowing unchecked now, but I didn't care.

"Shima did not say anything because Shima saying anything would not fix it. Shima would still die soon. And if Shima said something earlier, then Kunet would be sad longer. This way Kunet was happy as long as Shima could manage." He started to cry, and I hugged him to me, burying my face in his fur so he wouldn't see how shattered I was. "Shima is so sorry. Shima does not want to leave Kunet broken."

We held each other there on the rock for a long time before finally heading back.

The next few days I could barely focus on anything and stuck to Shima like a limpet. I was intensely aware of every change, the slightest hitch in something he would do, the momentary tremor in his gait. Even though they were barely there, to me they were as noticeable as if he had painted them upon his fur. And they swiftly became more and more evident. He was weakening, and though he still managed his typical playfulness and was energetic at times, I knew it was only a matter of days. He knew it too.

On the fourth day after he had told me, after I knew my life would change forever, I woke up just before dawn to find him missing. I was alone in the hut—I had insisted we not make the trek up the cliff path any more with his increasing weakness—and I called his name but heard no response. Panic overcame me then and I ran outside to find him, my tears making it hard to see. I desperately checked all of our favourite places, to no avail. With nowhere else to look, I started along the beach. The sun was coming up when I finally glimpsed him in the distance, wading in the ocean, slowly making his way towards me.

I sprinted towards him and splashed out into the sea. I was so focused on him that it took me a moment to realise he was pushing a small raft ahead of him. He looked exhausted, and he stopped when he saw me, his ears flattening.

"<Sorry, Kunet, this took longer than Shima thought. Not very strong right now>," he admitted.

"What... why a raft?" I stumbled over the words.

"Shima built a raft several moons ago, when Shima was strong. When Kunet was busy, or asleep, or writing on barks. Shima knew Shima did not have much time. Shima hid raft in bushes on other side of island, so Kunet would not find and ask Shima and be sad."

"Why?" But I didn't want to know.

"It is for Kunet. If Shima is gone, Kunet will be broken and alone. Kunet should take the raft and find Kunet's village again," he explained. He saw my expression and sighed. "<Please, Kunet. Shima does not want Kunet to be alone>."

"Oh, Shima..." I said sadly. I could say nothing else, so I motioned him towards the shore. "I'll push it, Shima. You're tired."

The sun was well within Aea's realm by the time we reached our section of the beach and I pulled the raft up onto the sand. I made Shima sit at our old firepit while I went spearfishing. To my frustration he insisted on being the one to build a fire, but it wouldn't have done any good to argue with him.

He didn't manage to eat even one fish, and neither could I. My heart hurt so much.

"<Kunet>?"

I shifted closer to him so I was pressed against his side.

"<Kunet? Shima needs Kunet to do something important>."

"What is it, Shima?"

"<Come, Shima will show Kunet. Over here>," he said, and he got up on shaky legs and headed down the beach a short ways to where he created his pigments. I followed closely behind him, should he stumble.

"<So, important things>," he said, gesturing to the rock and his coconut shell bowls of pigment. "<When gnolls... die...the *kishpsibi* paints special lines. It is so the gnoll can reach the spirits, and become a spirit themselves. Kunet! Do not cry, this is important, please>."

I nodded, unable to speak.

"Please, Kunet. When Shima dies, paint lines for Shima. No *kishpsibi* here, so Kunet has to do it."

And with ears flattened, he told me the designs to paint.

"Shima, I'll do my best," I managed.

"Will be easy. Gnolls not move around much when dead, remember?"

"Shima!"

"Sorry, Kunet. Shima makes jokes, Kunet knows that." He gave me a sad smile.

I led him back to our hut; he must have been completely worn out from the raft, for he curled up on our bed and fell asleep almost immediately. I held him a while, then got up to scratch a few more words on a sheaf of bark. I felt there was little need to write much more—all I had written since the very beginning was all that was needed, and I had no more words to share. So, I collected all the sheafs and placed them neatly in a pile, setting them in a corner, the knife resting atop them.

I was done.

Departure

"Some endings are merely beginnings."
Gnoll Proverb

I lie beside Shima, his back against my chest, and listen to his soft breathing. He's still tired, yet I desperately want him to be awake so I can be with him just a little while longer. He stirs, and I move to get the waterskin.

"<Shima? Are you thirsty>?"

He sits up and smiles at me, nodding. I hand him the waterskin, and he drinks all of it. I refill it from one of the coconut halves. The sun has already set, and the blue of dusk paints the sky.

"<Are you hungry? Do you want dinner>?"

"<No, Shima is not hungry. Kunet should eat, though>," he insists.

"It's okay—" I begin, but he interrupts me.

"<Kunet should eat, and Shima will sit with Kunet>." He gets up and pauses, standing on the threshold of our hut. He moves over to where the little statue sits along with the shell amulets and crouches near it, running a finger over it.

"<Shima still thinks Kunet made the sheath too small>," he grins, and starts off towards the beach. I follow.

I quickly fish; I only need food for one, and I have no desire to leave Shima alone. He sits there, limned by the fire's glow, a dark silhouette. I eat quietly and Shima sings, and I am glad the darkness hides my tears.

The stars are out now, and we sit in silence for a time.

"<Kunet...>" Shima says quietly.

"<Yes, Shima>?"

"<Shima wants to watch the stars with Kunet>," he says.

"<Shima, are you... sure>?" I ask, uncertain. He has been so tired.

He doesn't respond, but stands and takes my hand, and begins to head towards the trail leading up the cliff. I stop him.

"<Shima... let us stay here. On the beach. You are tired, the path is difficult, and here we will still see the stars>."

Detachedly I notice it's another full moon, like our very first time. We stand there, looking out over the ocean and the moonlight scattered upon the waves. I reach towards my other half and stroke his muzzle. His hands find my loincloth, untying it, and lets it fall. I do the same for him. We lay down together, and he turns toward me. Gently I set my hand on his chest and push until he is on his back, his face touched by the moonlight.

"<Shima... let me>."

I kiss him, lingering there at his muzzle. Then, bit by bit, I work my way down, softly kissing him at each step, and his erection slides free of its sheath. I kiss his tip, then take him in my mouth, relishing the taste of him. Slowly and unhurriedly, I work him, his quiet moans causing my own arousal to stand proud. I can feel as it builds for him, and it is not long before he gives a long low groan of ecstasy, my mouth enveloping him still, and he begins to pulse. I hold him there, my eyes closed, the taste of his release so familiar to me now. As his spasms slow, I let him slip from my mouth, and lick him gently as the rest dribbles onto his belly. I move back upwards to kiss him, and he kisses me gently and deeply in return.

Straddling him now, I reach back and direct him inside me, shuddering as he stretches me. I begin to move back and forth, sliding him almost out then deep within, again and again. He licks my face and whispers my name as he shudders, and I feel his heat spill inside me. I continue to move, his semen leaking from me as I coax more from him. When he finally climaxes once more, I do so with him, spreading hot over his chest. I embrace him tightly to me, our seed mixed together between us, as his pants slow and become the softer breaths of sleep.

I hold him there a long time, listening to his breathing, until finally I fall asleep too.

Dawn has already arrived by the time we awaken. Shima smiles at me, but it is plain there is a deep weariness to him. He is not hungry, but insists I eat, so he sits by the firepit as I fish. I cook some for him, in the hopes he might eat.

He does, but I think only to mollify me.

I had collected some kava and nightroot, but he refuses it. He says he is in no pain, but I leave them there by the firepit, just in case.

The day is cloudless and blue. The sea glitters.

"<Shima, come rest with me>," I plead, seeing his exhaustion. I sit on the soft sand and hold him close, my arms around him, cradling him to me with his head against mine. I grip him tightly as if it will keep him here, my face buried in the fur at his neck.

"<Kunet>?" he says, so tired now, and I let him know I'm there.

After a while, he starts to sing—it is breathy and barely audible, but I still sense it through his body. Eventually he trails off, and I feel him take one last, long, sighing breath as he finally relaxes. I can see nothing for my tears.

I lie there, lost, clutching my half that is no longer there.

Eventually, I am able to move and lift my head from his tear-stained ruff. The breeze plays with his fur.

I head to fetch the bowls from further down the beach, my thoughts absent. I feel too broken to think, so I just go through the motions. I find myself back by Shima, paints in hand, so I gently roll him on his back so I can begin to draw the lines that Shima described to me.

A yellow circle upon his chest, his centre.

White lines from each limb, connecting at the circle.

A white line from his sheath, a purple one from his forehead, and it is done.

I sit there, pressed close to him, and my vision blurs as the sky slowly darkens.

My vigil remains, and the stars accompany me. I watch as they turn in the sky, yet I barely notice. I hope it has been enough.

Dawn breaks, and it is a while before I realise it. Shima's raft is still here, and I stare at it for a long time. In my village, we say farewell to our dead and yield them up to Û's grasp, and so I lift my other half and pull him across the sand to the raft. He is much lighter than I expected.

I am reminded of dragging him from the raft when we first arrived, and I am overcome; I stop until I can begin again.

He is atop it now, and silently I push it into the ocean. There is no other home for me, and so I wade out, guiding the raft ahead of me, and I let it go.

I stand a long time, as it recedes into the distance, bearing Shima's body away. But there is no one beside me this time; I am alone.

A night comes, and the stars watch. A dawn comes, its beauty a proclamation.

The sun lowers once more, and its colours threaten to yield to another night of distant, lonely ancestors.

There is a flicker, a feeling ever so faint. A shifting in the air by the firepit at which I now sit, a refraction, a shape, a barely discernible image. It crouches there, on its haunches, and the soft pinks of sunset are visible through it.

It looks so much like him that my vision blurs once more.

He is closer now, a whisper in the air. The breeze stirs the sea, and I see the waves ripple through his form. I breathe his name, and he reaches out a hand.

I so desperately want to take it.

He shows me how. It is so very simple.

I have all I need. I paint the lines.

And, one by one, I untie the tethers that hold me here.

Now unfettered, I grasp his hand, solid now, and he is full of colours I have never seen.

I leave my broken shell behind.

Shima holds me close, and the island stretches out before us, awhirl and magnificent and impossibly vibrant.

And we join it, together.

Acknowledgements

Mostly, I write short stories.

Rafts is my first venture into a longer format story, and originated from a pair of NPCs I had created for one of my D&D campaigns. I then had this idea for them, and they quickly grew into a story and world all of their own. If you're reading this bit, it means you've probably finished *Rafts*, and if so, I truly and sincerely hope you liked it—the characters mean a lot to me, and I hope you enjoyed them too.

There were many who helped me along the way, and I want to thank them for all their support, both technical and moral. There were several who provided both a thorough readthrough of the story and excellent feedback, including Slip-Wolf, Domus Vocis, Huskyteer, and Joaquín Baldwin. Thanks to NightEyes DaySpring as well, for not only his feedback but also his constant pestering to keep pushing and complete this story. And Valerie, for reading all of my writing, not only *Rafts*, and being a fan of both it and my worldbuilding.

Also, many thanks to Chutkat for all the wonderful artwork, and for drawing more Shimas and Kunets than anyone should have to.

And of course, thanks to my wife Kikivuli for both her thorough proofreading and her unwavering belief in my writing.

About the Author

Utunu is a painted wolf who has been pretending to be a writer for several years. By day he is a game developer and has been working in the industry since the olden times.

He enjoys reading, boardgames, commissioning artwork, nature, tabletop RPGs, ancient history, obscure languages, conlangs, worldbuilding, proper football, linguistics, and the Oxford comma.

He has a few short stories and poems published, and his story *Water* received both the Cóyotl and Leo awards in 2020.

Utunu resides near Austin, Texas with his wife, son, daughter, too many pets, and several Kallax units filled with boardgames he wishes he could play more often.

mapakuvillage.com